Christopher Kenworthy was born in Preston in 1968, but has lived all over the UK. His short-story collection *Will You Hold Me?* was published in 1996 by The Do-Not Press. He has written more than forty stories for *Interzone, The Third Alternative, The Time Out Book of Paris Stories, Year's Best Horror* and many others. He now lives by the Swan River in Western Australia. *The Winter Inside* was his first novel.

Also by Christopher Kenworthy and published by
Serpent's Tail

The Winter Inside

The Quality of Light

Christopher Kenworthy

Library of Congress Catalog Card Number: 2001092081

A complete catalogue record for this book can be obtained from the British Library on request

The right of Christopher Kenworthy to be identified as the author of this work has been asserted by him in accordance with the Copyright, Patents and Designs Act 1988

Copyright © 2001 Christopher Kenworthy

First published in 2001 by Serpent's Tail,
4 Blackstock Mews, London N4 2BT
website: *www.serpentstail.com*

Typeset by Intype London Ltd
Printed by Mackays of Chatham plc

10 9 8 7 6 5 4 3 2 1

To Chantal

Acknowledgements

Special thanks to all those who contributed to the *Pilotage* film (based on *The Quality of Light*), especially Melissa Booth, André Bourgault du Coudray, Chantal Bourgault du Coudray, Elyse Bourgault du Coudray, Geoff Bourgault du Coudray, Graham Bourgault du Coudray, Natalie Burbage, Sarah Bowden, Alison Jackson, Richard John, Kingsley Judd, Danielle Lauren, David Loan-Clarke, David Meadows, Helen Merrick, Ken Morris, Tim Nickels, Justine Purdue, James Ridsdill-Smith, Nicola Ridsdill-Smith, Heidi Shukralla and Brooke Stafford.

Many thanks to my flying instructor, Colin Ekhart. Thanks to the many pilots I've flown with, especially Shirley Harding, Lewis Huang, Trevor Jones, Min Stokes and Don Woodward. Thanks to all at Minnovation and The Royal Aeroclub at Jandakot airport, and to The Beverley Soaring Club, WA.

Thanks to Jim Driver for publishing my short story 'Pilotage' in *Will You Hold Me?* upon which this novel is based.

Thanks, as always, to my friends and family, who offered support throughout.

Contents

1 Conflux   1
2 Scintilla   14
3 Ichor   75
4 Phlogiston   147
5 Reflux   203

1 Conflux

In late February I went down to the Jubilee Bridge after closing time to watch the drunks coming home. There were three pubs on Walney Island, but people went over to the mainland in the belief that Barrow could offer them a better time. Experience had shown me that they were frequently wrong, and they'd come back in misery. It was raining that night, the road shining with light from the town. Boats in the channel rattled with the sound of rope and metal, but even in that weather people were walking without coats, shirts flapping in the wind until the wet made them cling.

There weren't many good vantage points on the Walney side of the bridge, so rather than trying to be covert I stood by the traffic lights, pretending to wait for a friend. The first group of three passed me without words, heads down, earrings glinting where water pearled from them. I looked back at the opposite coast, dominated by the huge Vickers building, a six-segmented slab of ribbed concrete. Behind it, the sky was low and matt with streetlight. The rest of the town was difficult to make out, a mixture of house lights and silhouettes.

I was beginning to regret my decision to come out. My original intention had been to get an early night, but unable to sleep through the cold I'd chosen to embrace it with a walk. I wanted a clue, a hint as to what was going on. Impending spring made me believe something was about to happen. Even though the air was still sodden and gritty, snow tenaciously preserving litter and leaves in piles on the footpath, I felt a sense of spring and expected something to change. It was hope as much as intuition.

Around midnight I knew that I would either have to return when the clubs closed or call it a night. The few people I'd seen were quiet, or chattering about the weather rather than the way they were feeling. That was disappointing and unusual. Although people are bruised with cold in February, their emotions are ripe. It's usually a good time to hear them air those feelings.

I'd learned to follow drunken people, listening to their speeches. Whether they walked in groups or chanted to themselves, they talked mostly in gibberish, slang and obscenity. But if I listened for long enough, somebody would move to a higher level and say something mystical. It might not mean anything to them at the time, or would be lost by morning, but for me those words were treasure.

You see people acting in imaginative ways when they're in a state. The fury of a man walking home – pissed off, pissed up, dangerously upset – is a potent force, an energy that shouldn't be wasted. Sometimes they'd walk on the bridge railings, not for bravado, but to scare themselves. It wasn't alcohol, but a decision to step aside from the ordinary for a while. You could call it reckless, but I saw it as empowerment. It's impossible for that sort of action to go unnoticed; it changes the world.

There was a lot of anger in Barrow, some towards Vickers, most towards the Tories. Wherever people laid the blame for their misery, they took it out on each other. When people fought, it wasn't just to get it out of their system, but to hurt an opponent. Those urban myths about people sucking out eyes, and taping Stanley knives together (so the wound won't knit), all originated here. There was no cunning involved, no need to ask if a pint was spilled or a stare established; the fighting simply emerged from the presence of people. There was a rage that could be relieved only by flattening somebody else.

I'd read somewhere that anger and hatred come from a fear of stasis, but in Barrow people were angry because they knew things were changing for the worse. The whole place stank of piss and booze. The puddles of sick that coated the footpaths on a midweek morning made getting to the dole queue tricky. Everything got tackier, troubled by another layer of scum. The kids grew up vicious and gobby, and nobody gave a shit. People said it was the same everywhere, but I couldn't believe that was the case. There had always been an added tension in Barrow, because everything revolved around the submarines, which were — to say the least — volatile. They would fire up their nuclear reactors inside that fifty-foot concrete slab before slipping them into the sea. Nobody talked about safety, because nobody believed in it. When outsiders came into the pubs asking about the submarines, somebody would usually stop them going too far. Sooner or later one of them would remind us we lived on the most radioactive coastline in the world, asking us about acceptable levels. That's not something people cared to chat about.

There was a saying about living on the edge, which locals used from time to time. Visitors assumed it was something to do with the fear of an explosion. In truth, it referred to living on the coast, building a town against the waves, but in recent years it had summed up the poverty. The whole place was one great bargain bin. *Don't ask the price: everything's 50p.*

Some good came out of all that. Barrow may have appeared to be slumped, but, inside, the people were on fire. That energy had to go somewhere.

I'd spent most of my life in Barrow-in-Furness, but it hadn't done me as much harm as you might imagine. If anything, the opposite was true, because it gave me a chance to see things clearly. Had I taken up opportunities to travel I'd have been distracted by difference. Spending so many years in one place, coping with the same views, you become attuned to seasonal shifts and smaller changes of mood. When almost nothing changes, you notice everything that does.

When I was young I didn't like buildings being knocked down. Each time a shop was boarded up or a factory gutted, it felt as though my history was being diluted. It wasn't the dereliction, but the loss of icons. The most ordinary places became precious to me once I knew they could be lost. Two years after I learned to swim, they razed the municipal pool. It occurred in stages through the winter, the space it left revealing a surprising amount of new sky, and a blue-tiled hole among drifts of shattered bricks. I've never been one for trespass – being nervous of discovery taints the pleasure of a location – but even in those days I would take the risk to gain an image. One Christmas afternoon, when the house was quiet (my family boozed up and sleepy), I walked around the perimeter of the council site. It wasn't the deep twilight that I prefer, but a pale cloudy blue, exactly the same colour as the pool. From where I stood it looked as though the sky was melting into a space in the ground, so I moved closer, pleased to see that the pool held water two feet deep. Streetlights came on, putting a pink gloss on the tiles as the sky darkened. Among the rubble I found the stone footbath, the puddle it cradled faint with disinfectant. Beyond that I saw the concrete outline of the changing area, looking much smaller than the room had been. It amused me to see such an open space, knowing I had been naked there.

I was bothered by the significance of things. Sometimes when my dad was away at the weekends, Mum would take me to the bird sanctuary at the southern tip of Walney. We lived well inland, so the trip over the water was a treat, like a minor holiday. Looking back at our town from the island, the stretch of concrete and cranes was distant enough to be worth gazing at, silver steel chimneys reflecting in the channel's silt.

There was a flat headland, roughly mixed with pebbles and sand, all strewn with feathers and dry grass. Masses of seagulls peppered the sea and shore, a constant motion between the air and earth. The horizon was blurred that day, so it was difficult to tell where sea and sky met, and the water was so still it looked frozen solid. There were hundreds of dead birds among those that were nesting. They were lying on their bellies, wings wide and cruciform as though in flight, heads resting on one side, eyes closed. My mother walked ahead; she was wearing a red duffel coat, her hair, the same colour as the surrounding straw, blowing back around her face. There was sunshine there, so that against the greyed haze she appeared to be lit up.

When I stopped to examine a seagull with a torn belly, trying to determine whether this was the result of decay or a brutal death, I found myself staring at the curls of its intestines. In drying out, the stomach had swollen into a crimson pearl.

With her back to the sun, it was difficult to make out Mum's face, but I imagined there was concern. She pushed her hands in her pockets, wrapping the coat tighter.

'It doesn't mean anything, Marcus. It's just a dead bird.'

The walking began years before I had any idea what it could achieve. Mum worried, but Dad tolerated my disappearances, even at night, because getting shut of me was better than having me bring loud friends home. They thought I was hanging around outside Spar, and I didn't see any point in putting them right. Better to have them think I was smoking and drinking, rather than wandering alone.

My walks could last for hours, but they were always within the confines of the town. In the early days it was little more than voyeurism, many of my treks taking me down the canal towpath for the rows of uncurtained bedroom windows. It was only when I walked without planning a direction, trusting that I would be rewarded, that I found the best views. I'd pause to examine things closely – tinsel embedded in soil, the remains of a cat – and would eventually see something that mattered. I wasn't looking for beauty or meaning, but for images that seemed significant. I'd read somewhere that people used books as divination, randomly putting their finger on a line to answer questions. That had never worked for me, but walking until the world revealed itself did. With too much expectation or need, I'd find nothing. Only by walking calmly would I find an image that helped me know what to do.

The weather rarely stopped me, and that did get to my dad. If I came in soaked he would yell at me, not because he feared for my health but because it hitched up the laundry bill. It's fortunate that my walking gradually became more of a night-time activity; if I got wet, at least I could go straight to bed when I got in. Sometimes he'd make me do that anyway. He followed me upstairs once, laughing at first, then telling me I'd have to stay in my pyjamas all day even though it was early afternoon. He leaned against the doorframe, smoking, blowing the fumes into my room, chuckling again before he left me to get undressed. It rained until dark, the clouds bright orange, so thick and still I thought there was no chance of dispersal. I huddled in bed with the lights off, listening beneath the rushing mix of wind, shower and distant sea, trying to hear the impact of individual raindrops. When I woke in the night my curtains were open, the cloud gone, and the sky so starry it took me a moment to realise what I was looking at. The weather had never changed that quickly before, and the stars had never been so clear. I got out of bed and went outside, stepping from foot to foot on our tiny lawn, the grass so wet and cold my feet were soon numb.

Dad must have heard my rushed exit, because the hallway lights came on and he came to the front door with a torch in his hand.

'Get to bloody bed,' he said, trying his best to shout while whispering. 'It's the middle of the night. You've nothin' on yer feet.'

I hardly ever defied him in those days, and surprised myself by saying, 'Look at the stars.'

Instead of getting mad he just shook his head and refused to look at the sky.

'They'll still be there tomorrow,' he said.

The only other time I saw stars that clear was on the first night I went out with Andrea Walker. It was January 1981. I was fourteen, and she was two years older. She went to the other school, the one where they gave you high marks for colouring in your titles. Overweight and hidden beneath at least two jumpers, she wore jeans so tight they made her legs appear swollen. There was always a tang of sweat about her, which I came to associate with sex. I'd never even kissed a girl before Andrea, but she pushed my hands up her top the first time we were alone; I was as thrilled by the hard wire of her bra as I was by her breasts.

During that wet spring we huddled in bus shelters, feeling each other up. We spent the whole of the summer locked up in my bedroom, with the curtains drawn, getting pissed on cider and giving each other oral sex. Mum and Dad let us get on with it, because, as Dad once put it, 'At least he's not gay.'

I've never understood how I managed to withdraw so completely. By my fifteenth birthday I was pale and unwilling to see my friends. I'd learned a cycle of dependence with Andrea in which we argued, cried and made up on a regular basis. We talked about having babies, because half her friends were already pregnant. I started saving up for an engagement ring. What did I imagine married life to be like at that age? The two of us in a room, in constant need of a bath, listening to records and bringing each other off?

A few times my dad said I should have been with my

mates, kicking a ball. He probably had a point. At the very least I should have been outside again. I'd even developed a habit of keeping the windows closed, preferring our own body-stuffed air to the relative fresh from outside.

Despite spending almost every hour in a darkened room, the strongest memory I have of Andrea is from a day we spent outside, just before I started fifth year. Her mum and dad had taken us to the Lakes, and when they left us alone for an hour at Tarn Hows we walked into the trees away from the path so she could suck me off. It was warm and bright, and I was shocked at how much colour there was in my dick when it was glistening with spit, because I was used to seeing it in shadow. Worst of all, Andrea was competing with the flies; every time her mouth moved up the shaft, flies would buzz on to my wet skin, lifting away as her lips squeezed down. That was the only time I felt disgusted with myself, because we were surrounded by mountains and trees – the light itself seemed autumnal as though the colour of leaves had stained the air – and all I wanted was to come in somebody's mouth.

We were together for over a year, the break finally coming because of a dream. There was an irony in that, because I hated dream interpretation. It was a crass simplification of something vast, with dream dictionaries distilling massive narratives into vague symbols. A symbolic dream would have bored me, but instead I dreamed of feelings. I was older in the dream, sitting on the grass, outside what seemed to be a café, talking with a woman. She was a friend, and I loved her. It got sunnier, the light concentrating in her hair. It felt so real that for years after I believed it might come true. It never did, but that wasn't the point. The dream alerted me to feelings that could never have occurred if I'd stayed with Andrea.

I dumped her over the phone as soon as I got up, and she immediately came round on her bike. She looked panicked and hot, and I felt such relief that I laughed. I wasn't laughing at her, but I felt so good it was difficult not to smile. She hit me in the face and my nose burst. Where I swung away from her, I flicked a trail of blood on to the wall. Dad sent her home while I went to the bathroom, and once I'd got over the shock I spent the morning cleaning up the blood.

Six years later, when we took the radiator off that wall, there was a trickle of blood dried on the wallpaper, still quite red. For a second I remembered when she'd hit me; the smell of her nylon anorak, the blue glint of her bike in the background. I hadn't noticed those details at the time. It was as though the moment had remained in place, even though I'd moved on.

The problem with seeing so much significance is that you become greedy for meaning. More than anything, I wanted to feel things, and the aftermath of that year with Andrea made me desperate for a more emotive relationship. I felt so much when I was on my own, it was only logical that I should be able to expand those feelings by sharing them. Until I was nineteen, I made sure that I was always going out with somebody. The problem was that each time the initial emotions of being with a new girlfriend calmed I'd feel so stale that I'd start arguments. A night of drama was preferable to boredom.

It was baffling to see how fickle my feelings were. Within days of splitting up with people I'd felt love for, I wouldn't even think about them. There wasn't enough passion to make me bitter; I'd simply move my interest elsewhere, aching for somebody new within hours. It was as though love occurred in me with whoever happened to be around.

All of this was in opposition to my beliefs. I was convinced that nothing mattered more than real love. If I talked about the subject with friends, I was always the one saying that you should live according to your feelings.

Despite such lofty aims, my life was a bit of a mess. After three years at the polytechnic I'd moved back in with Mum and Dad and used my degree to get a job selling coffee to bad-tempered shoppers in the new food court. I stuck it out for six days. Nothing specific happened to make me leave – there's no incident I could pin it on – but it became too much and I walked out. Dad would have gone mad, so rather than tell him I'd spent the next few days sitting in my car in various lay-bys on the coast road, watching the weather. At night, agitated from having done so little, I'd walk.

It wasn't the employment prospects that were getting me, but a feeling that something had to change if my life was going to amount to much. I'd never been a miserable person, but felt utterly exhausted and melancholy. I was going out with Caroline, a student teacher from Carlisle, and wanted to get everything off my chest. Feelings, I explained to her, were all that mattered.

'Whose feelings? Yours?'

'What do you mean?'

'We're always hearing about your feelings. Do you have any idea how often you say *I*? *Me this, me that, I think this, I feel that.* It's all you ever talk about.'

'But . . .'

'It doesn't matter what you feel. It's how you treat people that counts.'

You get this image of yourself as kind, caring, feeling more than anybody else, and then you find out you're a selfish twat. It's like the face you pull to yourself in the mirror. That's an expression nobody else gets to see. In the real world your cheeks are never so thin or your eyes so bright. When you catch yourself in an unexpected reflection, it's surprising how flabby your expression can be.

My instinct was to argue, but I knew Caroline was probably right. For all my talk of passion, I was using people as a way of gazing at myself.

It was later that night, some time in February 1989, that I went down to the Jubilee Bridge. Standing in the rain, I watched the wet tarmac change colour in the glow of the traffic lights. The clouds parted to reveal black sky, almost starless around the full moon. A silver-grey contrail left by an unseen 747 had arced from the south. A dim star slipped from beneath it, the contrail moving away at surprising speed. The next time I looked up the trail was spread like cirrus, serrulated and dragged over the moon.

I felt even colder and decided to watch the lights go through their cycle three more times, and then I would go home.

A car passed, its headlights dead, one indicator flashing. I couldn't see the driver, because the windscreen wipers were off and a gauze of droplets obscured the glass. When its sound faded I could make out voices, but looking down the bridge there was only one man. He was talking to himself, his voice low then breaking into crying, which made it sound like there was more than one person. I didn't take much notice of his face, because I saw a fibre of pain drift from the back of his neck, setting in the air like a thread of heat haze. The trail of distortion was narrow where it emerged, but then blossomed, less visible where it widened. I backed up to the wall, but he saw me and put his hands over his face, wiping down to clean his expression as much as the tears. His big sigh must have helped, because as he passed in front of me the last of the thread came free, fading as he walked away.

2 Scintilla

Patrick came round for me before it was even light but was happy enough to wait while I showered. It was cold for October, and although the water had barely heated up it turned the air in the bathroom foggy. The sun was rising, so I switched off the bulb and watched the blue window-light turn rubescent as I dressed. The cold wouldn't have bothered me once, but the summer of 1995 had been the hottest I'd known, and I'd forgotten what it was like trying to keep a house warm.

When I went downstairs Patrick was poking around as usual, flipping through my books. Wearing his long coat and Docs, he could have looked like an overgrown art student but managed to appear well dressed. In the same clothes, I'd look like I'd slept in them. He had the sort of glossy hair that did what he wanted it to, just by running his fingers through it. I was envious of the fact that he could put on black jeans and a jumper, advocating scruffiness, but still looked like one of those men from an advert. He'd just turned thirty, but hadn't even flinched, probably because he looked five years younger. He smiled at my arrival, closing a hardback with a thud, indicating he'd found something useful. I knew by now that he wasn't scanning out of interest in the subjects, but to examine what I was reading. He was looking for ideas to test on me. Sometimes he'd throw out an obscure fact, days after having gleaned it from my books, to see whether I'd been paying attention to my reading matter.

'Anything interesting?' I asked.

'Of course,' he said. 'Ready? Your hair's still wet.'

It was freezing outside, the sun just catching the tops of trees, its flame caught in the leaves that remained. I hoped it would warm up soon, because we were going to be out all day. There was no rule that said we had to make such a thorough search of the town, but we felt better for putting in a full day's work. Before we set off I made a comment about the fuel being low. Patrick ignored me, feigning extreme concentration as he pulled out. When he stopped at the lights by the Jubilee Bridge, I looked at the spot where I'd stood six years earlier, that first night. I passed that place almost every day, but couldn't see the space without remembering what had happened to me there.

Patrick looked past me, down the length of Walney Island. You can't make out the airfield from there, only the sandbanks and slag heaps beyond it. He was weighing up the sky, checking the weather, trying to guess how much flying there would be today. When we'd first met, before we were friends, he used to give me meteorology reports as we drove; wind direction, cloud cover, base heights, advancing fronts and changes in temperature. It was partly to fill the silence, and before I knew much about flying I was impressed. It was only when I first listened to the Air Traffic Information Service that I realised where he picked up the daily spiel. After that, he gave up on his game.

'So, what's the weather then?' I goaded.

'No weather today.'

The thin, sunny cloud was shallow and ribbed, so that it looked more like a glare of ice. Diffused, the light was bright but unable to form shadows, which made the general grime and litter show up more.

On the mainland he drove up the west road. The Lucas garage was situated on a bend, pushing it against the coast. It was one of the few garages left where they served you, so we stayed in the car waiting for somebody to come out of the cabin, wondering if it might be Katie Oswald. She worked most Wednesday mornings, but we were greeted by the owner's brother, Fernleigh. He was a favourite with the kids around here, because he had no voice box. They would cycle out of town to buy sweets from him. It served as entertainment for them, to hear him struggle with simple greetings and prices. Some cancer or other had caused his larynx to be removed, and a whirring prosthetic had been jammed into his throat, which people said made him sound like a Dalek. That was a crude description, because the sound was more like somebody purring through a fan. A string-knit scarf was folded around his neck to disguise the wound, but that served to make you imagine it was more grotesque than a simple hole. His head was bald, fat and brown, and I always dreaded being served by him, because his gallant efforts to speak were incomprehensible. The fuel cap was on my side, so Patrick passed the keys to me and left me to deal with it. Recognising the car, Fernleigh lumbered over to the passenger window, knowing the routine.

Once I'd given him the keys and wound the window back up, Patrick said, 'Get out, you ignorant sod.'

'What's the point of having service if I stand in the cold with him?'

Patrick looked down at his legs, hunched. 'I should get this heater fixed.' We listened to the fuel going in, then he said, 'Ask him where Katie is.' He had a way of making me react to his suggestions, and I found myself standing outside the car, watching Fernleigh squint at the fuel meter.

'Is Katie around?' I asked, smiling toward the cabin, even though I knew the answer must be no, otherwise he wouldn't be there.

'Mhorning hoff,' he grunted, repeating it immediately to make sure I understood.

'I thought she always worked on Wednesday.'

'Bhak Ihater.'

'Fine, fine,' I said, handing him the money.

When I got back in, blowing into my hands, Patrick said, 'She must be getting sick of us turning up here every week.'

'I doubt she's even noticed.'

It was impossible to know how much she'd picked up on our attention. In the months we'd been aware of Katie I'd spoken to her only a few times, commenting on little other than the weather. She probably thought we were ordinary customers.

It's difficult to recognise a moment of change. If a lifetime of habit leads people to be set in their ways, speaking in stock phrases, waking up in a predictable mood, eating the same foods, what is it that allows them to change? Sometimes there's an accident, revelation or illness, some extreme that gives you the option of transformation. They say that astronauts come back to earth stained by the experience. The debriefing focuses on figures, procedure and process, but they're struggling with the beauty of what they've been through. The size of the earth stays with them, and whether they choose religion or seclusion, everything has changed.

As Patrick pointed out, however, some people come back from space unaffected. And when we'd taken people flying, some would be changed for ever, but others would claim it was just like driving. Perhaps it wasn't the moment itself, but a willingness to accept it, that made a difference.

If you try to work out why people are like they are, it can drive you mad. Even choice itself is influenced by every other choice and experience, so it's impossible to find the cause of anything in isolation. Some people would have you believe that your whole life is defined by the way your arse was wiped for the first time. If you end up beating children and screaming at traffic, it's nothing to do with what's happening in the real world; it's all down to your history of anal pressure. Others say we're fluid, changing according to every whim of circumstance. The problem with any of these theories is that even when you read whole books on them, they are incredibly basic. The people you know are rarely as predictable as they should be. Sometimes they do things, and you just can't fathom why. They change for no obvious reason, as though a gradual change has been occurring within.

That's how it felt when my renewal came about. It wasn't a change so much as the acceptance of an intense perception that had always been with me. When people open up to the world, it comes inside. The accumulation of images builds to the point where you can either choose to shut the perception out or embrace it. The change isn't always instantaneous, but it is persistent. Like with snake venom: the more you struggle, the greater its effect.

For Katie Oswald, change came from the drip-feed of observation. When I first saw her she was eighteen years old, pumping petrol at the Lucas garage. It was a summer of cloud and misty heat. Nobody was sunburned, but we all went brown, progressively dyed by the light. We'd squinted for two months against the stiff air, storing white in the creases around our eyes. At night, when relaxed, the lines came into view.

Spending time at the airfield, Patrick and I felt the weather more than most. There were almost no buildings between us and the horizon; although we could see the mountains and the town, they were less relevant than the grasslands that led out to the ocean. We felt open to the air at all times, acutely aware of the vast space above us.

Humidity meant that the sun was always merging with the fuzz around it, and gliding was limited that summer because of the haze. We took advantage of dusk when the worst of the smog settled below three hundred feet, roasting in the brightest sunsets I'd ever known. Sometimes we grew restless in the afternoons, or Patrick's students would pester for air-time and we'd take the risk. It was difficult arguing about bad weather when we were sweltering through the best summer for over a decade. Ray Shenton, the Scouse tow-plane pilot, was keen to build his hours and would bully us into going ahead. Every time Patrick was talked into it, he would come down angry. 'Frightened myself shitless,' he said calmly when the students were out of earshot, describing how he'd been unable to see the ground for the first minute of descent. 'But you should have seen the sea. Just like metal.' He looked disappointed with his description, but I knew what he meant. From ground level the sea is only a slither in front of you, and even the best sunset is a narrow smear of brightness. As you gain height the horizon rises, the sea opens and spreads below, wider than you'd imagine possible, gilded with miles of sunlight.

Patrick frightened himself too many times, and as the drought brought deeper misting and finer dust, we grounded ourselves more often. When Shenton pestered, Patrick took to calling him a 'Scouse twat' to his face. Shenton was a bony man, his chin always at the same stage of grimy stubble, giving you the impression he must shave in the middle of the night to avoid looking clean. He wore a white shirt, because he thought it made him look like a professional pilot, even though it went unwashed for a week at a time.

The summer remained a white glare into September. Although there were areas of blue sky, it never cleared fully, until the day I met Katie. It was her first day at the garage, and she spent most of the time outside, taking in the view. The clouds collected over the horizon of the Lake District, sucking on to the mountains, leaving the sky over Barrow as bare and blue as winter. The sea is grey at best, sometimes black with sewage, but on that day it reflected the sky, giving the illusion of Mediterranean waters. The sun was clear and sparkly. Staring up at it that morning, I realised why children draw it with rays all around it. When your eyes water, the light spreads out of it that way.

Sunlight as bright as that can make the most beautiful people unpleasant to look at, because it magnifies their skin. You can see the pores and hairs, freckles and discolorations, or the sticky layers of concealer and foundation. On Katie the light was like a layer of warmth, making her look well. It took an act of will not to stare.

She worked occasional evenings, and although we made no conscious effort to time our visits to her hours, we came across her more often than we did any of the other staff. On the few occasions when I found something to talk about, she was busied away by other customers. If she spoke first, Patrick would turn his head just enough to show that he was listening, so I didn't want to be drawn out. It was disappointing that we never found the chance to say much more than thanks to each other. After two months her face was as familiar and interesting as a friend's, but I knew nothing about her. On a warm September day, when Patrick was still working, he lent me his car and I drove up the coast road and parked at the Lucas garage. The weather was almost exactly the same as on our first meeting, unusually warm for that month, clear to the lungs, smelling of grass. It reminded me of how much time had passed and how little we'd spoken.

'I wasn't expecting to see you,' she said, as she put the fuel in. Surprised by her statement, I waited for an explanation, which she gave by pointing at the sky. I got out of the car, to see the glider overhead, mid-turn. 'It's been up at least twenty times today,' she said, topping the petrol up to the five-pound mark. 'I thought it must be you and your friend.'

Katie turned nineteen at the end of that month, and was upset when her squint lines became permanent. Having been free of oil and spots for less than a year, it was distressing to lose her youthful sap. She spent more time looking at those lines than she did at the good parts of her body. The more they grew, the more she rubbed in potions and creams. There was so much to celebrate about her body, I'll never know why she focused on the problem areas. She described her hair as brown, belying the fact that sunlight had turned layers of it blonde. That she left it unstyled, hanging at shoulder length, made her stand out. The fashion in Barrow was for a tight perm, to match an angry face. You got the feeling that most women wanted their hair to look damaged, as though they were tempted to shave it off.

The time she spent in the Lucas garage was as valuable as any other. She would sit in the cabin, behind her cash register, rocking back on the stool, watching the forecourt. When she was outside with a customer, leaning away from the worst of the fumes, she'd look over the beach and sea to the northern length of Walney Island. Beyond the black hangar, she could see the control tower, the wooden shack of the clubhouse, and a couple of caravans. Lined up by the taxiway, the bright whites and reds of Cessnas and Pipers. The orange windsock was often stiffened by a westerly. Two of the runways were hidden in wild grass because they were parallel to the coast, but she could make out the foreshortened blur of runway two-four.

It was a quiet airfield, most of its traffic being from Patrick's gliding club. Katie liked watching the aeroplanes land, and listened for the soft thump of tyres a second after she saw the dust and smoke of the contact. She watched the tow-plane take the glider up, but couldn't see the cable that connected the aircraft. At that height it looked as though the glider was formation flying. When the latch was released – the tow-plane diving to the right, the glider climbing to the left – she could see the tension between them break. The glider appeared to change shape in the turns, from white to a black needle, re-forming as it swooped around. Sometimes she would lose sight of it completely until it came in on finals, air brakes jutting out of the wings. There was a throbbing sound and a hiss. She thought it must be the same with all aeroplanes; the wings are singing, but you never hear them because of the engine.

Back in the cabin she smelled liquorice, melting chocolate, oil and polish. They had always been there, but her senses were coming to.

On hotter days, when the clouds crafted themselves to storm size, the glider circled beneath, taken up by rising air. When it was cool, with wind from the west, it flew out to Black Combe – the first mountain of the Lake District – gaining lift from the ridge winds. If the air was still, as it was for much of that summer, she saw the glider home in on Vickers, using heat reflected from the concrete submarine-house to buffet itself higher.

The Saturday after we first met, she worked late, given the responsibility of locking up and taking the keys home. For the first time she stayed on until dark. The forecourt gave off warmth, and the petrol smelled clean. There were two floodlights on either side of the garage, each cancelling out the other's shadows. She stayed outside, enjoying the lack of customers. She could hear the sea and spotted the tow-plane coming back with the cable, releasing it on to the strip before dropping to touch down.

The glider's flight was short, diving straight back into the circuit because it was going too dark. Katie didn't know, but the pilot wasn't trained for night flying. Patrick was using the legal limit of the daytime flying-definition to squeeze in his last flight. As he came in, the fog of town light contrasted with the dark island, so that he couldn't make out the airfield's features. The tower was closed for the night, invisible apart from the red tip of its beacon. He used the coast road to get his bearings, then lined up on the tyre-smeared numbers of runway two-four. It was difficult to judge distance, but as the house-sized numbers slid beneath him, he brought the glider level, losing sight of the horizon in the round-out. Knowing he could still be twenty feet up, he pulled the wings up almost to a stall.

I was watching from outside the clubhouse, but Shenton was oblivious. He'd taxied to the hangar door, killed the engine, and was winding on the wheel-brace to drag his aeroplane inside, while Patrick was flying blind towards the unseen runway. I looked at the hangar, the tail of the plane moving inside, then back out to the glider. Patrick was flying slowly, air brakes on full, but pitched in steep. I thought he was getting it all wrong, flying into the ground, but he was using the angle to get a better view. When he lifted into the flare he was too high, but not dangerously so. The drop gave him momentum, so that after the first impact he ballooned, then came down again. The contact helped him judge what was going on, if nothing else, and he kept it level. When he was down, he used his speed to roll up the runway. By the time I reached him, the glider was coming to a halt, one wing dipping to the tarmac.

You really need three people to move a glider safely, but we were the only ones left. Shenton was leaving in his Land Rover, driving so slowly we could have signalled for him to help, but we let him go. We each took a wing handle, promising to keep it slow. There wasn't much we wanted to say until the glider was manoeuvred into place, and then we leaned up against the hangar doors to force them shut.

It was warm as we walked towards his car, but the shock must have stiffened in Patrick, because he was struggling for breath. Being parallel with the coast of Barrow, we looked over.

'I've never been so glad to see the town,' he said. 'I knew it could go dark quickly, but I wasn't prepared for that rush of night.'

One of the lights at the Lucas garage was turned off, and Patrick watched with me as the other went out.

Knowing my preference for clearing the middle of town before we went to the outskirts, Patrick agreed to a quick wander through the centre. There were a few regular places I wanted to check on my own first, so I told Patrick I'd meet him in an hour and headed towards the Lamb.

The cold made my lungs feel heavy and sore, and I squinted at the unrelenting dazzle of clouds. We don't perceive the real intensity of light, otherwise the brilliance of a winter sun at midday would baffle us, and we would be blind at night. It's the ratios that count, the way one state relates to another. We can read by the light of a single candle or just as easily by the sun, which is a hundred thousand times stronger, because our eyes readily adapt. Step into a dark room and the eye manufactures visual purple; move outside and brown pigment floods the cells, protecting them from overload. This keeps our eyes safe, but it takes a while to adjust between these states.

The stone walls of the Lamb were bright at that time of day, and it looked dark inside. At night pubs are all you can see in the middle of town, their windows spangled with bottle light, but during the day they blend in among the shops, like foreign banks. You see them, but they don't register.

Pub doors rarely have handles, so when they're locked

they feel like part of the wall. I knocked, hoping the muffled thud would be audible inside. Ian McKenna's parents ran the Lamb, and although we weren't close friends I'd known him since he was in the fourth year at school. That meant I was served easily at night, and could return in the day to clear up the aftermath of an emotional night. Inside the pub first thing in the morning, among the polish and ash, there were traces of anger. Where the low sunlight ripped through, it revealed threads in the air. That's where the world had been damaged by somebody's pain.

Ian had never trusted me fully during my visits, and would wander in and out of the main lounge on the pretext of moving a chair or distributing beer mats. He must have had this image of me slotting myself beneath a gin dispenser and opening the valve. The truth was more mundane; I was clearing up the worst harm and I preferred privacy. Each time he came into the room I could do nothing other than look shifty. When he was gone it gave me only a few moments to soften my eyes, locate the fractures, and heal.

I'd explained this to Ian several times over the past couple of years, but he believed there was something vampiric about it, as though I was stealing energy to use in a ritual. I could never get it through to him that ritual had little meaning for me; it could break inertia, but nothing more. Even so, he was cooperative, and let me go through the process without a single refusal, keeping his parents out of the way, or explaining my presence to their satisfaction. The eagerness with which he usually let me in made me think he might have been afraid, not of myself, but of leaving pain in his building.

Ian took his time coming to the door that morning

and tried not to look at me when he opened it. He was dressed, but I got the impression from his tired face and the smell of smoke that he'd been up all night. His ginger beard looked grubby, as though he'd been rubbing it a lot. He ushered me in, stood by the bar for a moment, then left me to it.

I moved into the centre of the bar-lounge, in front of the fire, relaxing my eyes. A fibre of pain was strung across the room, like a crinkle of shining air. I moved towards the distortion. It became blurred, so I looked to the side, bringing it back into focus. It's the same technique you use for watching dim stars. If you stare at them they disappear, because the core of your retina is tuned for bright detail rather than night vision. By looking to the side and using a different part of your eye, the smallest stars are visible. The skill is to shift your concentration from the obvious centre.

The sunlight was diffuse and cloudy, but where it seeped through the distortion it sharpened like chrome. There's nothing dangerous about moving into the threads; the worst that can happen is that you'll resonate with the pain and make it grow. That sometimes happens when you pass through the scene of a previous argument. It returns, soils your mood, and the room becomes unpleasant, but that's all. Touching the fibres with the intent of sipping memories wasn't regarded as risky, but my real aim was to contain the event. By accepting the pain, I could heal this place. Sometimes nothing more was revealed than a smell or a word. Occasionally, I'd see the person who'd released the distortion or the event of their pain, as the thread was taken in and stored. This one moved quickly, so it was difficult to catch the memories, but I sensed somebody waiting for a car that didn't turn up, relentless rain. She'd come inside to dry off, and was alone when she least wanted to be.

Once I'd accepted the whole of it I checked for more distortions but found almost nothing; there were a few scabs of discoloration near the door, which I retrieved, but not much else. I shouted up to tell Ian I was going, and heard him on the stairs. He stopped walking and pretended not to have heard me, keeping completely still until I went out and closed the door.

There are so few trees in Barrow it's difficult to recognise the shift of seasons, except by the texture of moisture and the colour of the air. The ground outside Patrick's house was wet with rain. It wasn't deep enough to form puddles or wash away the grime, but formed a slippery coat over the footpath like dew. It rains every day in November, the evening colour stolen by long, blue twilight. When the sun does set it's difficult to see from the mainland, except as a rime of pinkish glow on the gasholders and chimneys. When there's high cloud, the sun warms the sky overhead from beneath the horizon. As I waited for Patrick to answer the door, the clouds went rosy, bright enough to make the tarmac gleam. His curtains were closed, with no light on inside, which concerned me as we'd arranged to walk to the Roundhouse. It was a week since I'd seen him, but I didn't want this to be another late night, so I knocked heavily, eager for his attention.

I heard him moving and saw his shape through the glass in the door several times before he opened it. I'd expected him to look tired or ill, perhaps half-dressed, but he was ready to go, his long coat on, and he smiled as though nothing was amiss.

'What's the delay?' I asked.

'I was getting dressed.'

'You could have let me in.'

'Whatever.' He smiled briefly, as though my complaint was irrelevant, so I let it go. He stood in the doorway, and I wondered whether he wanted me to go in or not.

'Are we off then?'

'I've some stuff to grab. Wait there.' From the kitchen he shouted, 'But close the door, would you? There's a draught.'

I left it open, hoping the cold would hurry him up. There was something bothering him, but I knew that even if he was completely honest he wouldn't be able to put his finger on what it was, so there was no point in asking.

The walk warmed us up, but it started raining as we crossed to Walney Island. Patrick ran the rain through his hair, brushing it back. It made him look smarter than usual, the water giving him a healthy sheen.

The road from the east to the west coast is a short one, passing through estates that give way to folds of dune and grass, the sort of place where you would normally expect to see a playground. At the road's highest point, where it splits down both lengths of coast, we could see the Roundhouse restaurant. Built mostly from breeze-blocks and curved, pebble-dash walls, the place was always dark. The sign over the door was no longer illuminated, and the red curtains were so thick no light came out. If we hadn't known that Patrick's girlfriend was working there that night, we might have had our usual debate as to whether or not it was open.

Inside it was bright, red lanterns on every table, the room gaudy with orange and yellow paint. It was meant to look golden, exotic, the counter adorned with a mixture of pot Buddhas, Chinese dragons and electroplated vases with dried flowers in them. It was Cantonese by name only, because the owner was white, and the cook was a black man from Preston, called Lennox. He'd moved here to be close to the Lakes, because he liked climbing mountains, although he admitted he hardly ever went now. We'd encouraged him to come flying with us, because he said he climbed for the perspective. And partly because we'd been enraged when our tow pilot, Ray Shenton, had insisted that flying was a white man's sport. For a start, flying isn't a sport, and although most pilots were white and male that wasn't a situation we wanted to preserve.

Lennox insisted he couldn't afford it, even though we told him it was cheaper than smoking.

'I don't smoke,' was his reply.

There was no sign of him that night. We were the only customers, and there was no sound of cooking. The restaurant smelled of bleach rather than food, but we headed for a table at the back, taking off our wet coats, hanging them on the chairs. Before anybody came through, Patrick stripped down to his T-shirt in an attempt to dry off. He sat back with his hands in his lap and looked off to the side while we talked. One of the first things I'd noticed about Patrick was that he rarely looked me in the eye, but in my direction, at my shoulders or hair, or other parts of my body. When he did make eye contact, it was brief, but you could tell that for him it must be significant.

We were whispering, as though being in there was an intrusion. There was always the worry that somebody would come through and tell us they were closed after all. It had happened before. When Suzette came in from the kitchen, she wasn't even holding a menu or a note pad. Whether she was working or not she generally dressed in black jeans and a T-shirt, her nearly blonde hair in a ponytail.

They'd met a year ago, three weeks after she'd had an abortion. On that first night she'd gone back to his house and let him come inside her seven times. Even when Patrick had been too tired to carry on, she'd propped herself above him and encouraged him to enter her. He'd been pissed enough not to worry about condoms, and chose not to ask about contraception until the morning. Taking that risk seemed to help her get over the abortion, but meant she was more reliant on Patrick than he'd expected. On the fourth night she said she loved him, and he'd worried about breaking up in case it upset her.

'I get on well with her,' he'd said once, 'but she doesn't care about anything.'

'If you meant that, you'd leave her. Besides, you're lucky to be with somebody who's so appreciative.'

Although I said that, I could tell why she disturbed him. Patrick sought beauty, and although he could see plain beauty in Suzette, it bothered him that she closed off to the world. Even if you pointed out something significant to her, she'd see only the mundane. You'd never find her enjoying a view, or a change in the light. You were more likely to find her sitting at the table with a cup of coffee and a cigarette in her left hand while she scribbled at a crossword with her right. She was good company, but shallow, talking forthrightly about sex as a way of creating apparent intimacy, rather than being genuinely friendly. She fidgeted and touched her face while she talked, raising the pitch of her voice at the end of each statement to make it sound like a question. She was in her mid-twenties but reminded me of a teenager. Even so, I didn't want them to break up.

'But I don't *feel* anything. I'm happy enough, but where does that leave us?'

Despite his complaints he'd seen her every couple of nights during the past year, and I knew that couldn't be just from an inability to break up.

She stood behind Patrick, smiled down at me, and put her hands on his neck, pushing her thumbs into the muscles there. I'd seen her do this before but it was peculiar to watch, because I rarely saw anybody touch him. Even when handing something to me, such as change or keys, he'd position his hand so there was no contact. Some people who don't like to be touched have an aura of tension, and huddle away, with rounded shoulders, limp handshakes and a constant fidget. Patrick, however, sat with his arms by his sides, an open gesture, which somehow made him less approachable. Pilots and mechanics who were prone to handshakes and back-slapping rarely made the effort with him, but if they lapsed you'd see something about him tighten.

As Suzette rubbed the muscles in his neck, I knew he'd be enjoying the sensation. His back had given him trouble since childhood, and they used to rack him up with weights and pulleys to straighten his spine. These days he often walked with his neck craned forwards, turning his whole body when he wanted to look around. Patrick's face remained impassive while she worked on him, and I thought that most people would narrow their eyes and make sighing noises, to express their appreciation.

'You're both soaking,' she said. 'Why didn't you drive?'

Patrick shook his head. 'Aren't you supposed to ask us if we want drinks?' It was the sort of comment that should have been a joke, but came out wrong. Nothing more was said but I could tell they were on the verge of an argument.

Suzette took our orders through to Lennox, then came back to sit with us while the food was cooked. Whatever tension there had been was gone.

'I had a dream last night,' she said. There were still only the three of us, but the room seemed to quieten the way it can in a crowded place when everybody stops talking at once. In that moment Patrick looked directly at me. Suzette was leaning towards him, hands cupped on her stomach, waiting for a response.

'Tell us about it,' he said.

While talking, she looked into the space between us, picturing the events.

'It was a flying dream. I was in an aeroplane, one with an engine, not a glider, but small . . .' Patrick nodded. 'It was over the countryside, in spring, far more beautiful than it ever is round here, all green and blue. But then the engine failed and we started to crash. The pilot was searching for a place to land, going round and round in circles.'

Patrick interrupted: 'Who was the pilot?'

'I don't know, I couldn't see him exactly. I knew he was there, though. He picked a field to land in, and we rushed towards it. All the way down I kept thinking it wasn't going to work, we were going too fast, out of control. We'd hit the grass and be smashed to pieces, or we'd clip the trees on the way down. It was frightening. But as the meadow came closer, the plane slowed, then it went to ground level, and I was just running on the grass. The plane and the pilot were gone, and I was running.'

'What do you think it means?' I asked, to prevent her from asking us.

'Nothing,' Patrick said, before she could answer. 'It was just a dream.'

'I thought, you know, just in case...'

Patrick shook his head. Her talk of crashing aeroplanes had annoyed him. When his students swapped stories about disasters, he would snap at them, because they couldn't enjoy flight if they were obsessed by danger. Although he was safety-conscious, and often lectured them on how to avoid accidents, he didn't like endless speculation about crashes. Sometimes he'd sulk to the extent of grounding the glider without explanation, until the students became anxious to get in the sky again. 'No more talk of accidents,' Patrick would say, by way of punishment, before taking the instructor's seat again.

There was quiet for a while after Suzette's voice trailed off, and I thought it might be left at that, until Patrick said, 'Besides which, you can glide without an engine. Forced landings are rarely fatal.'

Suzette was cross with him now. 'So you wouldn't be scared if the engine failed?' Then she looked at me. 'Would you be scared, Marcus?'

Before I could answer, Patrick said, 'Finding a safe field would be easy.'

'It was only a dream,' I reminded him.

'I'm not all that interested in dreams.'

That wasn't completely true. He used to take great interest in dreams, reciting their details to me each morning that we met. The problem was that his dreams were largely of emotions, which the images never communicated. He'd just keep telling me how much love or fear he'd experienced, exasperated that he couldn't convey their grandeur. There was one dream in which he'd been in a building with three friends. They'd been writing a book, by hand. It had red leather covers. They lit a fire on the floorboards, to burn the book, but it vanished when it touched the flames. Immediately, they hacked open a space in the wall, and found the book, charred, ten thousand years old. He was certain it was meaningless, but the feeling had been immense.

I considered reminding him, but I could see he was uneasy. He smiled then, and I could tell he was keen to prevent an argument with Suzette, but I wasn't sure why it had bothered him so much. He wanted to move on, but couldn't think of what to say.

The most memorable dreams are realistic, but the most impressive reality always feels like a dream. I was reminded of this one Saturday in October, two years earlier, when Patrick flew with his students from dawn until dusk. Suffering from the aftermath of a cold I didn't fly, but Patrick never tired. It was as though he was trying to break a record.

We were taking advantage of a cold, sunny day when there was no haze. For the first few hours the runway glittered with frost, then, as the sun melted it, with dew. There were no clouds, but even without a breeze it was freezing. I knew from experience that, despite the cold, we'd all be sunburned.

At midday the flights lasted up to half an hour, because they circled over the submarine building, using its reflected heat to gain lift. I'd keep the students occupied between flights, strapping them into the front seat when it was their turn. From the back seat Patrick would tell me a few details about the conditions, sometimes noting the tower's obsession with radio protocol. 'I've got air brakes on with my right hand, ailerons in my left, rudders full of crosswind, wanting to retrim, and the bastard asks me to report on finals. Which hand am I supposed to pick up the radio with? If he cared to look out of his palace he'd see I was *on* finals.' We'd look across at the control tower, its blue glass room like a huge, cheap sapphire.

After such an exchange I'd drop the canopy over them, check that the other students had connected the cable correctly, zigzagging it to the orange tow-plane. We'd cut the turnaround down to two minutes, and when Patrick was ready I'd level the glider and signal to Shenton, then run with the wing as he revved away. At that point the wing felt so flexible you'd think the smallest wind could snap it. Moments before I'd let go it would rise in my hand, as though waking up, the glider becoming light. There was enough flight in the wings to prevent them tipping back to the floor. The glider would rise first, suddenly fluid in three dimensions, the tow-plane lifting higher, settling to climb as the glider followed.

That afternoon I walked down to the landing point, just a few yards in from the sea. The numbers on the runway – three, five – were painted as wide as the tarmac, the white skidded with flecks of rubber. The tow-plane came in low, and detached the cable, and I ran out for it, looping it around one arm as Shenton touched down. He pulled off to one side of the runway and killed the engine.

While the glider circled at two thousand, I walked back to where the students were waiting. Nicola was standing aside from the others, watching the sky. She'd been for her first flight that morning, and although she'd been talkative before, she was silent now. Her dark hair was too short to be tied back, but long enough to get in her eyes. Refusing to use her hands, she tilted her head in and out of the breeze to clear it from her face. I'd wanted to talk to her, because she was the only woman of a similar age to me, and in some ways she reminded me of Patrick. It was probably because she was wearing a long coat and being quiet, but it was enough to make me want to talk to her.

Watching the glider slip on to the downwind leg, I asked her how she'd enjoyed her flight. Expecting the usual rush of babble from a first-time flier, I was pleased to see her face go smooth. The wind slowed, and the dull heat of the sun cut through the chill for a second, so much glare reflecting from the grass that it looked white.

'It was like a dream,' she said. I watched her mouth as she talked, because her lips were red like a child's, made darker by her pale skin. She told me about the stillness of the air, how she'd expected it to be noisy and rough. 'It made me weightless. Half of the time I forgot the glider was there. There was so much space.'

The glider's canopy is a plastic shell with no struts to obscure your view, and it comes down almost to waist height, so you feel like you're sitting on top of the aeroplane, rather than in it. At three thousand feet, you can sense the curve of the planet, the horizon frowning down in your peripheral vision. The wings bend higher than the cockpit, the sun's reflection sliding up them in the turns. Nicola had wanted to tell somebody about this, but amid the amateur dramatics of other students miming frights and mistakes, she hadn't found room. I was glad that she came to me, because I'd been in similar situations, unable to share what I'd experienced.

When we tell this story to people, we always say that Nicola never went back to work, that she committed to flying that afternoon and changed her life. It isn't quite true, because she weaned herself away from her job gradually, giving it up that autumn. She sold the house she resented and learned to fly. She worked on the same airfield, operating out of the small flying school on the other side of the control tower. There wasn't much work on Walney, she said, because few people could afford powered flight, but that didn't bother her. She spent her days near the aeroplanes, with a view of the sea and the mountains of the Lakes. I remember Nicola touching the cowl of the Tomahawk once, patting it as she said, 'This is my office now.'

Some people take years to emerge in your dreams, but others appear there immediately. I dreamed about Nicola the night after she first came to the airfield. Had I been younger, I'd have taken that as a sign that we were meant to be together. I now knew how easy it was to be misled by the emotions of a first meeting. The strongest feelings can be the least informed.

When you know nothing about a person other than the way they look and move, it's easy to feel something bordering on the mystical. There's no hope for a future, no imagined sex or love, but a feeling that it matters to be around them. I'd felt that way about Nicola when she'd spoken about flying, but didn't trust the sensation, because I'd known it to be wrong with other people.

The last time it had happened was in the aftermath of violence. Just about everybody in Barrow's been beaten up at some point, but John Gavaurin holds the record. There must be something about his posture, or the little round glasses, that makes people want to thump him. He'd get a kicking every now and then, but Patrick showed no sympathy, saying the only surprise was that it didn't happen more often. Having seen John cope quite well, I was surprised to find out how awful it felt to be in a hopeless situation myself. It was late on a Saturday afternoon when a group of sixteen-year-olds decided to attack me, because – from what I could work out – they saw me reading the *Guardian*. Maybe it was because they couldn't read, but they seemed to find the idea of somebody reading in public a great social ill. I made the mistake of trying to talk them round, and ended up being strangled to the floor and kicked in the eye. They ran away then, probably because I went so still. The attack left me in a fragile state, to say the least, so I went round to John's house, presuming he'd be able to sympathise. He wasn't home, but Sheila – the Scottish art student from the front flat – let me in and took me to her room, bathing my eye, talking, and then making dinner for me. It doesn't take much imagination to work out what happened. We were together for three months.

It wouldn't have lasted five minutes without the emotions of that first meeting. For whatever reason – the smell of the lawn, the wine we drank, the heavy sunlight that filled her room – Sheila and I had felt something. When it ended, neither of us really cared, and it was difficult to imagine how we'd bothered to spend so much time together. I couldn't even work out how we'd found the energy to argue.

Incidents such as that made me wary of asking Nicola out. It wasn't that I was afraid of the reality of a person. There's nothing wrong with the intimacy of farting and snoring and picking your nose in front of somebody. I didn't avoid Nicola for fear that she'd become ordinary or relaxed. My worry was that the emotion itself was completely misplaced, brought about by my own moods and needs, rather than the person she was.

Some time after she first flew solo, Nicola cycled down to see us at the clubhouse. Patrick and I were sitting on the steps, reluctant to go home even though nothing was happening. It was late August, but felt more like September, because high cirrus made the sun glare. The afternoon was tinted with haze. We swapped flying stories, and with the clubhouse to our back we didn't see the sunset, but watched the town and the mountains warm in its light. It was an intense hour, because we all had this relaxed demeanour, but I was aware of every movement and intonation she made. Sometimes she'd lean in to talk, and that would be enough for me to catch the smell of her shampoo. Other times she'd look off to the side while talking, pausing as she thought. Her smile was rare, because she often looked so moved by the things she talked about. When she did smile, holding eye contact for a moment before looking away, it felt like she was projecting her warmth. I found myself shaking my head at the way that made me feel.

By the time the air was turning blue I'd decided not to ask her out. Until then, my habit had always been to ask people out soon after I met them, if I thought there was any chance of it working. It's a response most people develop once they get past twenty-five. You don't feel you can afford six months of glancing at somebody, so it's better to get on with it. I might have done the same with Nicola if I'd felt less. If she'd just been attractive, I might have given it a go. But she stirred feelings that meant I'd be investing so much hope, it could only put pressure on us. Every slight setback would make it feel like something important was being undermined, and small arguments would become huge ones. I'd probably end up hating her because I'd feel incomplete without her. It felt wrong to nourish emotions that could debase me in that way.

The only thing that worried me was that by holding back I might be falling into that trap of admiring from a distance, which is just as unrealistic as trusting those first emotions. I could end up hoping and waiting for two years, only to go out with her once and find she annoyed me. Even worse, I might wait all that time and be turned down. Despite this, I resolved to keep my distance.

My decision was arbitrary, because a couple of weeks later she moved in with her boyfriend, somewhere on the southern part of the island. I didn't see much of her in the following couple of years. The few times we met she told me how she was progressing, and I enjoyed her enthusiasm for flying. It wasn't difficult being around her. The only problems I had were when I was alone at the airfield, on those days when the weather was still, with high cirrus and haze. I found that difficult, because you can't remember what you once felt for somebody, without feeling it again.

The weather never repeats itself exactly; there's always some minor change. That's why there are no dull days, even in Barrow, because there's always a different combination of breeze, moisture and cold that makes each day unique. When you look for the meaning in the weather, it presents itself to you.

If you pay attention to your senses, nothing comes as a shock. Whatever happens, no matter how unusual or upsetting, part of you thinks, *I knew it*. You hear people say this all the time, after accidents that came from nowhere, or when a faithful partner is caught with their pants down. It's nothing to do with subconscious doubts or body language cues; in the most basic terms, it's precognition. If you are aware of these feelings, and work with them, you can tell when something is going to happen. They are no use to you in hindsight, so you must learn to catch them before the event. Some people use the weather, others deal cards or throw sticks. Patrick and I had learned to read the town, the scatter of objects, the timing of slammed doors. In a moment of indecision, if a car alarm sounded, we'd know to back off. We never really went in for black cats crossing our path, but the more ordinary details of our lives rarely let us down.

Sometimes, however, I felt that Patrick went too far, and it was usually when he was in a bad mood. That night at the Roundhouse, we managed to keep the conversation calm once Suzette was busied with another table of customers, but I knew he was edgy. The food was rich, and we walked home stuffed, mouths hot with curry, teeth freezing from eating the free mints. Our footsteps were slow, but Patrick struggled more than me because of the extra wine he'd taken in. It was drizzling again, making the mainland appear foggy, the drops swelling in streetlight, so the whole town was blazed in orange. On the far side of the bridge I saw blue and red flashing lights, but there were no sirens. Whatever the emergency vehicles were gathered around must have been in trouble for some time.

'An accident,' Patrick said. He wasn't stating the obvious so much as showing distaste. 'What do you think it means?'

I couldn't answer and hoped he'd keep quiet. His question upset me, because I saw this as an event in itself, rather than a portent. If there was somebody trapped in a car, it was unfair to think the accident occurred simply to predict a change in our activities. At such times things stop being a symbol of what's happening, and are a symptom of it.

'I'd better go and have a look,' he said.

On the following Wednesday night, as we drove up to the fenced perimeter of the airfield, where the road narrows to the width of one vehicle, we saw a figure leaving the Crown. He was bathed in yellow light until the door closed behind him. It's the only building on that road, and the smallest pub on the island, feeling more like a front room with a bar. It was sometimes busy in summer, when Patrick's students gathered there to discuss their learning curve, but could otherwise be deserted. We were interested to see who was there at tea-time in October. He stood back from the road, scratching his shaved head as though to hide his face. When his round glasses caught in the headlights, I recognised John.

Patrick slowed down. 'What the fuck's he drinking for?' he said.

'Maybe he was early, passing the time.'

We pulled alongside him and Patrick wound his window down. John backed up a bit, leaned in. His skin was still bad, lips chapped to the point of cutting his mouth wider. The air stank of exhaust fumes and he grimaced against them.

'Want a lift?'

John licked his teeth, nodding, and headed for my side. When his window was up again Patrick had only a couple of seconds to whisper, 'He shouldn't be drinking when he's the victim.'

'Just leave him be,' I advised.

I got out, nodded hello, and John climbed into the

back seat. Patrick was peering on to the airfield, towards the clubhouse, avoiding eye contact with either of us.

'Are you well, John?' I asked.

'Well as ever,' he said. 'Better, in fact.'

I'd known him as long as any of the others, but John Gavaurin was a stranger. Patrick couldn't stand him being around, not from a personal distaste, but as a result of discomfort. John talked of almost nothing but our activities, in a way that even made me feel uneasy. His relentless questions and speculations were carried out in public places, or in the middle of unrelated conversations. If you tried to find out what else he was interested in, it always came back to this.

John had developed a knack of hogging my time. If I bumped into him when he was free, he'd want to spend all his time with me, and would concoct various plans to waste an afternoon. His technique was to offer temptations. Standing on Duke Street one afternoon before Christmas, I'd tried to explain that I had to go home; I'd been working all morning, I needed the rest, I was going out later.

John had looked at the ground. 'You need a pint then.'

'No, really, I just need a rest.'

'Maybe you're hungry.' As he'd said it I could smell the chips from Shep's Chippy. 'Come on,' he'd said weakly.

John made it difficult to say no. I didn't feel relaxed enough with him to say *sod off*. Instead I had to be firm, and these days after a few hours I'd tell him I needed the time to myself, which always seemed more satisfactory than an excuse.

In the car that night as we drove on to the airfield, he was quiet, probably nervous. I was also expectant, already feeling the process coming on. Against the blue sky I could make out the hangar, the control tower closed for the night, and the clubhouse. It looked like a sagging shed, every panel showing more grey wood than paint. Two of the walls were windowless, the other two made almost entirely of glass. We could see right through it to the ocean beyond the airfield, and, inside, the moving shapes of people. As the headlight passed over, splintering in the scratches on the windows, faces turned our way.

It was that night that Katie Oswald watched television in bed until the electric meter ran out. She'd been channel-hopping anyway. There was no point in getting up to put coins in the meter, because until morning she wouldn't need electricity. The fridge would be off, but it needed defrosting anyway. There was more ice than food in there.

The television screen retained a phosphorescent sheen. Staring directly at it she could see almost nothing, but when she looked away its square appeared like a flash. Her reaction was to stare straight back at it, which made it vanish. The rhythm of her pupils from side to side wearied her eyes, and they closed.

Human eyes are uncommonly sensitive. The minute energy of a single photon can register as light. When astronauts try to sleep, their retinas are bombarded by a background radiation that never reaches earth. Each particle activates an individual cell, appearing as a speck of bright; the effect is similar to staring at a television filled with static.

Katie saw a brownish, sludgy pattern moving chaotically, unaffected whether she opened or closed her eyes. It would be satisfying to see nothing, but the mottling remained. This reminded her of being sent to bed early as a child, when she would relieve the boredom by pressing her palms into her eye sockets, causing patterns to appear. By squashing the vitreous humour against the retina, she'd excited the cells. Imagination had played a part, twisting the entoptics into frames of colour and structure. She could have tried this again, but instead she observed the rusty darkness, wondering if it was a defect caused by her childhood habit.

As she drifted in and out of sleep, her dreams were dull and repetitive. Waking frequently, she was aware that time was passing, unsure of its rate. When the window filled with twilight, she guessed it must be around five o'clock. The colour of dawn is an illusion. In reality, all the colours are present, but our eyes are incapable of picking them up. The cells that respond to red are less efficient, and the world appears blue because blue is easier to see at low intensity. By sunrise, the colours in her room had returned. Red curtains and carpet, lime-green walls, her piled clothes a mass of creams; they didn't appear to be illuminated so much as heated with light.

It would be misleading to say that she felt fully rested, because her sleep had been too disturbed, but she didn't feel as shattered as usual. Sleep was a paradox, something she forced herself to do when wide awake, which left her feeling tired. According to convention, it was supposed to be the other way around.

That morning, her eyes were free of crust, hair feeling clean. When she dressed, her clothes slid over her flesh without any feel of stickiness. In the mirror, nothing had changed, but she found she was rubbing her hands together, the vigour making her uncomfortable.

The renewal is frequently accompanied by restlessness, a desire to do something extreme. For Patrick, his moment of opening was so unusual it left him desperate. Nobody can suggest exactly where the change in him began, but one afternoon in 1988 can be singled out as the time when the alteration became tangible.

Working part-time in two different pubs, while collecting a Giro, Patrick's needs were few. He lived with his parents in those days to save money, using most of his wage to keep flying. His other luxury was a red Fiesta, but on this he spent as little as possible. He believed that leaving petrol in the tank was wasteful, that twenty billion gallons of fuel were sloshing unused in cars every day. 'What's the point of leaving a fiver's worth below the red line,' he said, 'if you can run it to empty and get your money's worth?' So he carried a plastic can of fuel in front of the passenger seat, driving until he felt the familiar stutter and cessation of the engine.

At first this was nothing more than an inconvenience, as normal to him as refuelling at a petrol station, but in time it became a form of divination. Wherever he ran out, he felt as though he was being shown something. The code of these locations was unclear to him. Sometimes he came to a halt in the middle of a blind bend or on a bridge, and although there could be obvious symbolism he believed there was something more subtle to it.

He charted the locations on a map, to see if there was any correlation. He used a detailed OS map, rather than a flying chart, marking each incident with a black dot. Some of the locations did line up, but less spectacularly than he'd hoped. In time he decided it was possible there was no code, but that he was being shown each place for the sake of looking at it.

When you've lived in the same area for years, driving on certain roads becomes automatic; there are clear reference points which guide your driving. You know there are some places where it's safe to look at the hills or watch the sky. Other than that, all you see is tarmac, fencing, hedges and the distinctive roadside litter of shoes, tyres and baby bottles. If somebody else drives you, the same road becomes new. Where you normally watch the catseyes curve around a bend you can look to the left and see Highland cattle in a paddock you didn't know was there. Or a canal beneath a bridge, which you thought went over a railway line. Or a ploughed field coated with the smut of bone meal and milt, its powder shining like swarf. For Patrick, interruptions to his journeys were a similar opportunity. He was being given an excuse to pause and observe. While the petrol flowed from his plastic can into the car's tank, he was given a few seconds to take in his surroundings.

The fuel needle was unreliable; it could fall to its lowest point an hour before the last drops were used, or with a few minutes to spare. On some journeys he would take the scenic route, to ensure that he didn't make it home without a reason to stop. That September he went further out of his way, coaxing an event into being. He wasn't supposed to be driving, because he'd had his wisdom teeth out that morning. The anaesthetic had turned his blood to something like antifreeze, icy and sour, leaving him shaky. The only discomfort came from a strain in his jaw and the half-memory of clamps under his lips, so he'd refused the offer of codeine in case it wearied him further. With his wounds drying, and able to speak normally, he'd convinced them that he was being picked up.

He didn't want to go straight home, so he went out of town to the east as far as Kendal, then up the edge of the Lakes, curving back towards the coast. The needle hit the red line as he left Aspatria. When the engine hesitated, caught, then faltered, he knew that this stoppage would be special, because it wasn't a road he was familiar with, and the car rolled to a halt in a lay-by. It felt as though the crescent of tarmac had been spread there purely for his arrival. When the car was refuelled, he locked up and walked away, wanting to see beyond the immediate location.

The fields were delineated by barbed wire and gates, but there were no hedges. The footpath he located had no signpost and could have been private. Walking without a hedge made him feel exposed. The ache left his muscles, and the aftereffects of his operation gave him a feeling of resilience. He looked back for the car, but the road was out of sight. In all directions he could see fields, most set-aside, some containing overripe wheat, the heads drooping.

The path adhered to a river, but the stillness made it look like a winding canal, its varnished surface well below the banking. There didn't appear to be any variation in depth, and although the sun showed up a fine suspension of silt, he could see no fish, stones or rocks. There was none of the usual detritus of grass and plastic along the water's edge; the steep banks were too smooth with no rushes for materials to gather on.

Down the exact centre of the river, cutting ripples around itself, a smoking log floated towards him. It was a thick branch, almost a tree, the ends snapped away rather than cut, its bark all charcoal. It moved without sound, smoke coming out of the cracks. The log rotated around its length in front of him, betraying currents, settling again on its axis, following the curve of the river. When it was past him he smelled the burn of it, like water poured on a still-warm bonfire. Looking upriver he could see the stretch of fields, pylons, distant farm buildings. There were no fires, factories or trees, no smoke or activity to show where it could have come from.

The clouds were thin but dark, untouched by low sunlight, which made the landscape brighter. The pylons turned the colour of bulb filaments, the grasses beneath them overexposed. A scent of burning remained, but the log had gone, the water re-creating flatness.

By the time Patrick made it back to his car, the sun had fused over with even stratus and he was shivering. Already restless, he drove back faster than he needed to, knowing something had to be done.

Patrick's initiation came two years before mine. We were both discovered by Donald Beyer, who ran the control tower on Walney. If it wasn't for his sleeveless shirts and khaki pants, Donald would have looked like an ageing doctor: long face, immaculate white hair, raised chin. I'd never seen him smile or blink; the only betrayal of emotion came when he swallowed, his throat distended by a sharp Adam's apple. To an initiate, this calm made Donald appear stronger than he was.

When Patrick was brought into the process a few months after his experience by the river, he was anxious for control. The way he clung to Donald during those first days – asking more questions than Don thought reasonable – may have led to his later isolation. Few of the group were friends, coming together only for the rage, rarely discussing the nature of the activities. After his initial struggle, Patrick chose isolation, moving away from his parents and letting go of his previous friends.

All this lessened when he met me, because he was no

longer the beginner. There's something about newcomers that draws us to them. It's more than a sense of what they are, more than we gather from directed insights; coincidence brings them into our lives. Patrick was aware of me on several occasions before I had any idea what was happening to me. Even before my first sight of pain, he'd been watching me. Whenever he saw me he would approach, weigh me up, then back away. He never told me about this, but the afterglow of the rage can be used to gain insights into other people's points of view.

On a road behind the rugby stadium close to his house, he saw me observing a shadow that came off a lamppost. He could see that I was working out the way the sun was shining, trying to see why the shadow spread in the middle, where it should have been precise. Thinking back, I have no recollection of anybody else in the street, my concentration being on the distortion. If he had come to me then, and been my teacher, it's likely that we'd never have been friends. He held back from bringing it out in me because of his age, letting Don stumble across me instead.

He was wise to resist, because I was far from ready at that point, my perception barely getting beyond minor glimpses of damage. It took another few months for me to see things clearly. There was an avoidance of my new state, but I had an intuition that I shouldn't panic about the changes. It's been suggested that I resisted through fear, but I know it was more to do with wanting to be at ease with the situation. Although I've always sought a deeper perception, the distortions themselves were so strange I didn't want to stare at them in case my bewilderment made them vanish. I've always thought that awe is calm and quiet, nothing to do with gasping and heartbeats.

My renewal made me trust the process of being patient and accepting. I was right not to worry, because once the renewal was under way the sights that came to me were too intriguing to be ignored.

When Donald found me, I was standing outside the paper mill, trying to follow a thread of pain which tapered across the road to a bus stop. I don't know how long he'd been watching me, or how he became aware of my observation. He didn't look at me, but I paid attention to him because he was the only other person on that road, and he looked familiar, his white hair nudging at my memory. I was also aware that he was looking in the same direction, although his face was far from puzzled. Eric Street is a long road, the shore side enclosed by a wall so tall it hides the buildings behind; the sort of place you could feel trapped in at night. Even though it was mid-afternoon, I was aware of how frightening a road it could be. Donald moved slowly forwards, walking into the rippled wire, absorbing the form into himself. Only when the retrieval was complete did he turn to look at me.

He let me follow him to the clubhouse. It was a long walk, but I knew not to approach him or to ask about our destination. It reminded me of the walks I used to go on as a child, navigating to an unknown landmark simply by following a trail of appeal. It's easy to say this now, but I feel that even if he'd walked in another direction I'd have ended up at the airfield. Had the clubhouse been locked, I'd have been unable to resist breaking in. As it was, he took me there, telling me to wait outside for a moment. During the day the single-room building was cluttered with chairs, tables, empty oilcans and rags, but I immediately looked at the dusty wooden floorboards, visualising the space as cleared. Donald moved the furniture aside, making the space I wanted.

When the room was clear he let me in. Nothing was forced, but he led me into the rage.

When I asked questions afterwards, he refused to teach, letting me work most of it out for myself. He said that he didn't want to pollute my discoveries, but within a few weeks I realised his reluctance was more to do with a general unwillingness to talk, rather than an avoidance of our subject in particular.

In those early days I would hang around the airfield to help with the gliding club, so that I could be near the clubhouse, sometimes going to see Don or chatting with Patrick. Don let me stay in the control tower, watching traffic through the tinted windows. He observed radio protocol at all times, reminding the more jolly pilots to do the same, curbing their banter with commands. If I asked him a question about the circuit pattern, or the rules of flight, he'd advise me to watch and learn. It's a miracle that he was viewed as a leader, considering how unhelpful he was. It must have been something to do with his age and his appearance of calm.

I got even less out of Patrick at first, because flying was a subject that kept us occupied, allowed us to be together without having to talk about our other activities. I enjoyed being near the gliders, sprinting with a wing tip until the vibration of air made it lift from my hand. I loved running to grab the rope where the tow-plane released it on to the runway. When the glider returned, I'd strap the students in, lowering the canopy over them. Sometimes I'd stand with the students while we watched the glider in flight, listening to their expectations, their stories of earlier flights, trying to give them advice. Those who came to us with the greatest initial enthusiasm would usually have one flight, and they'd come down looking bewildered, and we'd never see them again. Others would learn to fly, get their licence, and then vanish. Nobody stayed with the club for more than a season, and this regular turnover of people drew me closer to Patrick.

I can't remember Patrick calling me by my name during the first months, so that when he finally used it I knew that something had changed. We established that our other activities should be put aside when socialising, and after a while the subject became almost unapproachable. Even so, we knew that without that connection we would never have been friends. By spending time together, we lessened the loneliness that keeping a secret brings.

There's no way a person can go this deeply into healing without a retreat. Carrying a month's worth of chaos dampens your mood, which is partly why we employed the rage. Nobody talked about what might happen if the pain was left inside without the cleansing. It was assumed that we needed a place to unravel the threads of disorder.

We didn't use pain as fuel for our workings, even though pain was an essential part of it. We weren't feeding off the damage so much as clearing it out and restoring stability. Any benefits we received were a by-product.

On every fourth Wednesday evening, when the airfield was quiet, we gathered inside the clubhouse at dusk. That was about the only symbol we permitted; twilight is a time of change. There was no elected hierarchy, no order of arrival, though I was often the last of the twelve. Once together, there was no ritual or invocation, no salt circle or scratched symbols. We used silence to release the anger.

Under normal circumstances, people are incapable of obtaining silence. Even when the creak of your guts fades, and traffic and breeze and floorboards are made quiet, you can hold your breath, still your heart, and there will remain a perception of sound. A humming tone, sometimes a whistle. These illusory whispers are the result of damage to the inner ear, caused by sounds so loud or continuous they have weakened a part of the cochlea that responds to them. As apparent punishment, a trace of that vibration stays with you for ever; it's the auditory version of a phantom limb. Age-related deafness is nothing to do with quiet, but the roar of past noises brought together at once, the collective memory of sound drowning out the detail of speech.

If you listen for long enough, while you drop off, this background rumble turns into music, singing voices and violins. It can wake you up, or be lost as you fall asleep. In our stillness, the same would happen, which is why even this frothing of our damaged ears was checked by use of the imagination. Once the rage was under way, sound returned, but to set it in motion we needed absolute silence. The other senses needed no restraint, which was fortunate, because the clubhouse was rich with perceptual distractions.

From the west we could see the last of the light coming over the sea, across the airfield. To the east there was the black shell of the hangar, the slag heaps on the mainland looking like sand. The walls were adorned with aeroplane posters, maps and charts, the crisped traces of old Sellotape patterning the wall behind them. It smelled of floorboards and paper. As the darkness thickened, the posters and hangings lost their detail, the gloss on them reflecting like grainy mirrors. For our workings, the table was moved to the side, the chairs arranged in a circle, facing inward.

As each member arrived, sea air was let in, then shut out. Each successive closure lessened the volume of sound. The night we picked John Gavaurin up at the Crown, we were the last to arrive, and moved to the three empty seats. With the quiet established, the twelve of us made eye contact with one another before becoming still. Outside it was dark, but our vision was catching up, and there was enough lambency from Barrow to keep the faces visible.

With each meeting the responsibility of being the victim was passed around clockwise. John had been chosen for this rage. He'd remained free of pain during the past weeks, because you can only cleanse pain that has been gathered by other people. He walked to the centre of the room, facing the direction of his empty chair.

Initiating the event took an act of will, in much the same way that blinking or moving your arm does. There's more than decision involved, but no effort. The victim had to be willing to accept the pain, and without force, we would let it go.

The air seemed to set, and my body trembled. As the threads emerged from us, I concentrated on John; if you focus on anything other than the victim, there can be problems. Dwelling on the pain can cause it to snag as it withdraws, leaving a vestige of distress that lingers for weeks. By losing everything to the rage I avoided contamination.

Although a victim is always visibly moved by the event, John was affected more than usual. His hands cramped against themselves, setting into fists, and he made steps to the left and right, sometimes backwards, staring at his fingers, which opened and closed with the waves of fury. His teeth were tight, lips drawn back, the strain in his face making the muscles solid. His arms moved away from his body and back with each clench, as though he was embracing something invisible and difficult to hold. A frenzied growl came from his lungs with each contraction.

The last thread left me, and I caught flashes of pain from the others as it wound into him. He leaned over, his face like a crying child's, grasping his stomach like somebody who had been winded.

We waited for the calm to take over. When the pain has pooled in a victim, it needs to be purified and dispersed; the victim has to let go of it. During the release we could take the energy back, give it direction, apply it in some way. By using the victim as an attractor, the others were unblemished, free to share and shape the power. That's why we'd been accused of feeding off pain, which was less than fair. Our purpose was to remove the suffering from Barrow. If we gained benefits from this craft, as a side effect, who could complain?

John straightened up, his lips pouting with the effort of looking composed, and he opened his mouth in a roar. The wave came off him like a summer wind, soaking into my bones.

Crouched by my bed, with curtains closed and lights out, I thought about Katie Oswald. The afterglow of rage warmed my imagination, and I pictured her face, close, sleeping. The insights had shown me that she was coming to her senses, but it was difficult to know how much had occurred to her. If I was to bring Katie into the fold, I needed to know more about her. I allowed energy to seep into the working, enabling me to look beyond her immediate situation. The problem with these images is that chronology gets mixed; you are just as likely to see the person five years ago as in the present. Although Katie could have no idea what I was doing, her wishes, fears and thoughts about herself would shape what was available to me. If she suppressed memories, or withdrew from events, they would be hidden from me as well.

I tightened my eyes, trying to allow an image of her recent past. The secret is to let the images come, rather than force them. It's like trying to unlock a door in a hurry. If you rush, the key just slips over the lock, or sticks on the latches, jamming the mechanism. The only way to make it happen smoothly, no matter how desperately you want to get inside, is to act as though you aren't in a hurry. I must have been trying to grab her past, though, because I saw her as a young girl, outside the stables at the south of Walney. Up before sunrise, her footsteps were sharp on the frosty concrete. She could smell cold straw, creosote and the grassy breath of the horses. The gloaming gave way to a sky of white, chilled haze, the sun rising red, its disc unable to colour the sky.

The image faded, frustrating me, because I needed to see her now, to determine how much awareness of our process she was gaining. If I went to her early, she might be frightened off for ever, but without guidance she could make regretful errors. Something like that had happened with John Gavaurin. Although Patrick and I had been aware of John, we'd let Don go to him first. Patrick had agreed with me that it was too long a delay, and I'd often thought I should have brought him on. Left to his own devices, John had been frightened by his experience. His nervousness continued to be a worry, and I'm sure that came from being left alone with his increased sensitivity for too long.

My knees were sore against the carpet, my back ached into a curve, and I could feel a need for sleep. It would be wasteful to use any more energy on Katie, as I had my own concerns. There were other ways of using the traces from our rage meetings: to reduce the need for sleep, for protection, to hold people away, even to attract them. Some people attempted to use the aftermath to see into the future, but I didn't have much faith in that. I preferred the divination of my senses, so I let the last traces be used in that way, brightening my perception further. When the moment was over, I looked back at the curtains, the moonlight colouring them like blood and ash, almost believing that I could feed off the light.

In December Barrow-in-Furness entered a state of twilight. The clouds retained a dark hue even at noon, streets shone with headlights and shop fluorescence. House lamps were left on by those who could afford to, and fires were stoked all afternoon. It was often foggy in the town, and I'd hear people complain about the dullness. To me, the fog was the same blue as clear sky, holding the light, strengthening it with colour. At four o'clock, just before the streetlights came on, the town looked its best.

Katie's awareness was growing, but in a way that made her uncomfortable. In previous years, December had been a month to get through, but now she was obsessed by its detail. She focused on the air, sensing the distance between objects and variations in colour. When she saw tangerine peel on a roadside grid, pith side up, she turned it over to reveal the orange, bewildered by its significance. On cloudy days she longed for the sharpness of shadows, and when the sun came through she examined the texture of concrete and stone, the massive intricacy of tarmac. She smelled the town, its mixture of marsh and oil and coughed-up air. Walking past a churchyard on Duke Street, she saw the green-wrapped buds on the alder tree, where next year's leaves were poking through. She'd always assumed new growth came in spring, like it says in the poems, but saw that the process began in winter.

She knew when the moon was waxing and waning, even if it remained behind the clouds. Sometimes she'd waken in the night, eager to draw the curtains back for a look at the stars. It was as though her sleeping body knew when the sky was clear. The intensity of observation was puzzling, but there was also the side effect of regaining her body. The cold in her fingers when she forgot her gloves was close to pain, the bones feeling like they were bleeding. Breathing cold air made her taste phlegm building in her throat and lungs. When she caught a cold, the fever turned to nausea and panic, her headaches powerful enough to keep her in bed. Her periods were no longer than usual, but they cramped from the skin inwards, her whole torso a fabric of tension. She was conscious of her smell, a lemony tang to her skin, but when she showered, the water was either so cold or hot that it stung. For days she was unable to find the comfort of warmth.

When you open up to perception, you are more vulnerable to pain. You become so aware of your body that the messages of its existence are exaggerated, and you feel permanently disrupted. There's a danger in feeling things too intensely. Our bodies required calm, because too much excitement tagged on to a sensation leaves the body open to infection. A small fear about your throat being sore can lead to its closing up. Katie learned about this one night when she was unable to sleep, because she kept swallowing and swallowing, feeling a thickness in her throat, as though it was turning solid, too narrow a slit to breathe through. After hours of discomfort, she realised that the future she had imagined was coming true, and that it would take willpower to change it. In response, she imagined her throat wide, knowing that the tension was her own. The squeeze eased, and with each sigh she gained more control.

During those weeks I saw little of her, because illness kept her from the garage. At that time I had no idea whether her renewal was complete, and was anxious to find out more. By Christmas she found the balance required for our methods; an intense experience of sensation, received calmly. Despite this, and the perfect conditions in the town − darkness and abandoned streets − she still didn't see a fully formed thread of pain. The closest she came was at dusk, when she took a short cut behind the Fraser Shopping Centre. There was a blemish in the air, but she mistook it for a problem with her eyes.

On a day that was almost too cold to venture into, following a freak snow from the east, I walked up the mainland coast. On a deserted pebble beach, Katie was stepping over plastic rope and wood that had been left by waves. I was cold, and I wanted to talk to her. It was windy, and she squinted against the bright cold. She looked around at me, but didn't smile or even acknowledge recognition.

Later, I was anxious for company, but Patrick was out, so I spent my time trying to find gaps in the walls where cold was leaking in. As I crammed newspaper wedges into slots in the plaster, I couldn't get the image of Katie Oswald out of my head.

Patrick rarely visited me at work, but walking into town I got a feeling that he would. The sun was low and there was a stinging wind; it was a combination I'd come to associate with his presence. From my road I could see the ocean to the west, like wrinkled foil where the sun broke on to it. As I crossed to the mainland, the channel was deep with rough water, the sway of the boats making them chime. In town, hard rain turned the air as bright as cloud.

On days like that the Arcadia Second-Hand Bookshop became like a library. The owner never came in, and I was the only member of staff, so I let the soaked and weary warm themselves as they pretended to browse. To make life easier for them, I'd read avidly when they were leaving, so they didn't need to skulk out. From the window I could see the Larches Estate, a place I'd always been reluctant to wander through. Retrieving pain is difficult unless you're alone and relaxed, which is unlikely on an estate where people carry knives as fashion accessories. From my chair I could see the smoke of daytime bonfires which they lit in the courtyard among the rubble of a demolished home. When the five-storey blocks were built, each was made of concrete slabs like marble, but a few years of rain and fumes turned them the colour of soot. Trails of washing were hung like bunting around the railings; the hollow metal was strummed and thumped relentlessly by the children who still had enough energy to charge around. They wore bright clothes made of glossy material, but their faces were sallow.

Children rarely came into the shop, but adults did, and

they picked up the books with pictures, glancing at each page for less than a second. Nothing much was sold that close to Christmas, because money was being reserved for presents, rather than second-hand reading.

Patrick came in after lunch, looking frozen, hands in his pockets to wrap his buttonless coat around himself. The leather of his Docs was trimmed with salt from the morning rain. His face was so cold it had gone pale blue rather than red. He said, 'Put that kettle on,' as he moved behind the counter and leaned on the radiator.

I loved the way he'd come round with a sense of urgency, but would then be relaxed enough to hang around in silence, rather than feeling obliged to speak. He looked at a crack across the glass-topped counter, a ribbon of mirror where a customer had leaned too heavily. He ran his finger along it, trying to feel the fracture, but the fault was internal. He went to the window, looking out at the Larches.

'Have you seen much of that girl from the garage?'

'Katie?' I asked, wondering why he referred to her in that way.

'Yes, Katie. You're still thinking of bringing her on?' he asked.

'Maybe. Why?'

'No reason.' He gestured over to the Larches. 'You know she lives over there, in the flats?'

'No, I didn't. I've caught glimpses of her room, but I didn't realise it was there. How do you know?'

'Something Fernleigh said, that's all. I'm surprised you never see her in here.'

Patrick poured himself a cup of tea and warmed his hands on it, staring at the light fittings. He took an interest in a paperclip holder on my desk, one of those magnetic efforts that held the clips together in a pile. For the next half-hour he experimented in silence, testing various theories as they came to him.

It reminded me of the time we'd taken his old TV to pieces. Things like that would only ever happen in winter, when there was no flying. He'd be left with all these empty hours which he had to fill with curiosity. Rather than read a book, he'd take something to bits whether it needed to be repaired or not. In the case of his TV, it had stopped transmitting pictures, but glowed and hissed, which made him certain that it could be fixed. We spent seven hours trying to dismantle it, and I've rarely known him so happy. If he'd been any good at what he was doing, or if he'd known what he was looking at, I'd have found the whole deconstruction a bit sad, but he hadn't a clue. When he exposed the copper wire, braided around glass, his eyes widened. To get that far into the machine we'd had to use an axe. No amount of unscrewing and forcing was good enough, so in the end we'd hacked the wooden shell away. He assumed that if we gradually wrecked the thing, we'd learn something about how it worked. Neither of us stopped to get a drink or go to the toilet, because any lapse in concentration might make us give up. The miracle was that we pulled wires and boards out, but the thing kept working. We were even able to get the picture back by locking on one channel. There wasn't much left to the TV, except the tube and a few attachments. Next to it, the splintered case was piled with the remnants of our attack. If it could work without all those extras, Patrick said, they must never have been needed in the first place. It was part of the capitalist conspiracy to sell stuff that wasn't needed. He promised to put it on display in public, to make his point, but the next time I went round it was bagged up next to the bin, hidden in frost.

Winter bothered me because it was difficult to keep him occupied. In flying he'd found some stability, but when the weather failed I found his intensity surfacing more frequently. On some days he needed no distraction, and could sit for hours watching the sky without talking. Other times, I'd cure his need with an afternoon of drinking or a long walk. But sometimes he reminded me of the way people say they're happy and coping, just before they burst into tears. He denied that, saying, 'It's better to be interested in the world than allow myself to get bored.'

Patrick's curiosity extended to people and places. He'd seek out the most frightening pubs and was willing to talk to the damaged people who frequented them. No matter how scary those places looked, he'd make me follow him in. There was one pub called the Fighting Cock, which looked more like a nightclub from the street, because there was just a door in the wall with no sign of windows. Even though we went in on a dull day, we had to pause to let our eyes adjust to the darkness inside. There was more smoke than light, even though there were only about six people in there. It would have been less frightening if there'd been a boisterous crowd. An old man in a greasy blue suit was sitting by the wall, talking with two men in leather jackets. A few others were sitting alone. You couldn't make out what was going on in the corners, but could just see the gleam of a glass or the rim of a table. You had to admire that place for resisting refurbishment, but it was far from welcoming.

'To think, some people come here to relax,' I whispered, once we'd found somewhere to hide with our pints.

It was because of his obsession with such places that Patrick went on about the Larches Estate. That afternoon in the bookshop, he kept bringing the subject up. I'd always argued against going there, saying we wouldn't be able to cleanse that area of pain without access to the rooms. There was no point in creeping around the balconies and passageways if we couldn't get inside.

'It can't be as bad as you make out if Katie lives there.'

'But I don't see the point.'

'If we only ever go to the same public places, what good are we doing, really? Why bother clearing out tame places when the real anger's happening elsewhere. Imagine the shit that goes on in there.'

I urged him to be quiet, because my customers might be listening, but he continued, saying, 'It's no wonder the Larches is so fucked up if it never gets cleared out. Anybody would go mad in there.'

When it came down to the practicalities, though, he had no answers. I said I'd go if he could think of a way to get into those rooms. Although he made some joking suggestions about pretending to rent a room, I knew I'd just about put him off.

'Still, it might be worth a wander.'

I managed to change the subject, and we arranged a time to go out for New Year. When a man came in asking me for the New Age section, Patrick waved and left. He stopped outside the door, perhaps trying to decide which direction to take, maybe just shocked by the cold, then leaned into the wind and walked away with his head down.

When I went home a couple of hours later, the wind had dried the rain, and gaps in the clouds moved rapidly, circles of sunlight passing over the estate like spotlights.

*

New Year was a washout, not just because of the rain but because we made plans and tried to have a good time. The pressure was on because Patrick had split up with Suzette a couple of days after Christmas; it had been his decision, but he was miserable about it, so we agreed to cheer ourselves up with a good night out. We, of all people, should have known better. It's common knowledge that the best parties occur spontaneously. If you try to make a night special, it usually disappoints.

I was wary of New Year because people feel so obliged to invoke a special event. The result could sometimes be exciting with a ritual of minor disorder occurring around the town hall Christmas tree; a few people would attempt to climb it, and mounted police would charge in. After the countdown there'd be this mass of kissing, with pissed girls moving from one person to the next. There'd always be a few huge men calling their girlfriends slags, pockets of arguments among the merrymaking. With so many police around the fights never picked up much momentum. That year, however, the police had nothing to do, because a persistent downpour meant most people huddled into their local pub and stayed there.

It was nearly a week later, when the decorations were due to come down, that we made up for it. Patrick and I hadn't even planned to go out, but he came round in the afternoon. There was a cold front coming in like a line of change across the sky; half was clear blue, the other a granular grey that promised snow. He stayed for something to eat, and by the time it had gone dark there was about an inch of snow outside. It was that that made us go out, so we were dressed for the cold more than a party.

There's a system of navigation known as pilotage, where

you find your way by flying from one landmark to another. Whether flying, driving or walking, it was the way we preferred to travel. Rather than planning a destination, we'd move towards the next point of interest and look again from there. We took this method seriously, because it was valuable to our workings, leading us to areas of dense pain and uncollected disruption that we'd never have found through logic. In our private time, however, it was also the best way to move, and we always had the best nights out by navigating that way. That night, we didn't even decide where to go, but walked according to the sights that interested us: children sliding their bikes on the school playground; a building site where orange lamps blinked randomly; one white streetlight, which illuminated nothing but itself and a snowy cone of air. Everywhere we walked there were a few scrapings and signs of activity, but always a hush, as the snow deepened.

We walked straight to the Lamb, because it was so close. Ian was behind the bar pulling pints, his ginger hair and beard looking almost blond in the glow from the Christmas tree. The windows were still crammed with silver tinsel.

'Bad luck,' I said, indicating the decorations as we passed the bar, and it took Ian a couple of seconds to realise I was joking. As usual, he looked nervous, especially as there were two of us together.

The pub was busy, but our favourite place was a round table in the middle of the lounge, which was usually left free. People prefer to inhabit the periphery of pubs, but we liked it because it gave us some distance from the video game, the bar and the toilets. We could hear ourselves think, talk without being heard, and we could observe the whole pub.

Patrick went to the bar and Ian served him silently. In the nearest corner, a group of students from the art college tore up their beer mats, leaning in to each other as they chattered. I felt a slight twinge of annoyance at the way they looked: the layered clothes, the dreadlocks and friendship bangles, the little round glasses, Docs and overexcitement. And then I realised I was actually feeling jealous, because they were at that stage where you never go out in groups of fewer than ten. There was something to be said for that, and seeing them reminded me of how easily friends dropped by the wayside. I wasn't cynical enough to assume the same would happen to them, or to frown at them for downing their cider in races. They weren't using alcohol to tame themselves, or to impose a false experience, but to speed their emotions. Alcohol makes you believe that what you imagine might come true.

You could see it in their faces, the need. They didn't realise, but they were reaching out to each other with every joke and laugh. I wasn't even drunk, but I was feeling affection for them, even the ridiculous boys with little tufts of beard. That in itself made me feel older. I'd become maudlin because I'd rather be with a big, mixed group, getting pissed in the hope of getting off with somebody.

Patrick returned with a pint and a double whisky for each of us. It was his favourite way to drink; sip the whisky, warm it down with the bitter. He pointed over to the corner.

'Nicola was there,' he said, 'while you were daydreaming. And she was with Katie Oswald.'

'Nicola from the airfield?'

He said yes, but couldn't explain how she and Katie

might know each other. That was the last they were mentioned in that hour, but something had sunk in. Two people on the outskirts of significance had been seen together. It was probably a good sign, though I wasn't sure of what.

When we spoke about it later, and tried to analyse how we ended up at the airfield that night, Patrick said it was because of the snow. Without that, he claimed, we'd never have wanted to make the night last so long, or have headed out to the coast; there would have been no need for the view. I never agreed with him, and I think he was gently taking the piss by blaming the weather. Besides, I don't believe the future is so sensitive to initial conditions. I think we'd have ended up there whatever we'd intended, not because of fate, but because we were all so open to the occasion. Feelings can be more powerful than cause and effect. The mood that arose once the four of us were gathered meant there was never any way we could have gone home separately.

Even a couple of days later, it was difficult to recall the exact sequence of the evening, partly because nothing particularly dramatic happened. If anybody else had tagged along, they might have said it was a dull night. After all, we ran out of booze and had to sleep in the cold. But Patrick and I still found ourselves mulling over the details for days. We disagreed on the order of events – probably because we'd been half-drunk – but managed to agree on a general impression of what had happened.

When we'd been drinking for an hour, Nicola came over to say goodbye, even though she hadn't said hello.

'We thought you'd left,' Patrick said, then trailed off with, 'or we'd have . . .'

She drew up a chair while she waited for Katie to get back from the toilet, and explained that when Patrick had first seen them she'd only just met Katie. They were there for a mutual friend's birthday, and because they'd been the first to arrive, they'd sat together. Now, as the others were going to a club, the two of them were going to share a cab home. While that was registering, Katie came back and sat down, and before Nicola could introduce us she said, 'I know these two. I see them at the garage all the time.' We then swapped names, and she said she knew, because Fernleigh had told her.

Patrick rose to go to the bar, and we all accepted his offer of a drink. There was no debate between Nicola and Katie about whether they should stay or carry on home, and it felt as though they'd planned to be with us all along. I knew that wasn't the case, but within minutes it felt like we did this with them all the time.

The conversation was easy, but I'd been drinking faster than I'd realised. When I went to the toilet, I found myself breathing carefully through my nose to avoid throwing up. Given the cold smell of crystal disinfectant from the urinals, that wasn't easy. I washed my face in the freezing tap water, a reminder of the night outside. Staring into the mirror, I saw one drop of water swell on the end of my nose, then tumble off. I used the hand-drier to warm my face, but had to keep my eyes open or I would have fallen over.

Heading back to our table, the rest of the pub looked frantic and tense, but there was a stillness around Nicola, Katie and Patrick. Although they were talking eagerly, and sometimes over each other, they appeared calm. I realised as well that Nicola and Katie were the only women in there without make-up. It made those around them look saturated with colour.

While I'd been away a decision had been made to make the trek over to the island, to get last orders at the Crown on the edge of the airfield. With so few customers, that pub was likely to stay open for us past closing time. When we went outside, however, the snow was so deep that walking looked unlikely. Overhead, the sky was breaking, orange clouds rimmed with blue moonlight. It had stopped snowing and was getting colder, but we stood in silence, trying to work out what to do. I think we were all worried the night was going to collapse.

There was only one live car on the street, a snow-coated cab with the engine running. The driver was an Indian, and as soon as he set off he told us he'd never even seen snow before, because he'd lived in London for the first few years he was in England. He expressed surprise at the way the car kept getting away from him, sagging sideways, being straightened by the kerbs as much as his efforts. We remained quiet, to let him concentrate. Crossing the bridge, he took it slowly, but the car felt like it was floating across rather than being driven. On the other side the snowed branches of the trees were all clear and highly defined. As we passed down the island, the view was made hazy by our breath on the windows.

I thought back to the way Nicola had made me feel, two years previously, and knew it would be easy to let those feelings rise again. She was in the front seat, looking out of the side window so that I could see her profile. In the dark I could only make out her face from the headlights reflecting off the snow. Her dark hair shone where it had been wet by snow, and there was damp on her neck. I willed her to look back, to make eye contact, but her eyes kept casting over the view.

The taxi driver dropped us at the Crown and drove away carefully, the wheels spinning and sliding, but the engine sounding muffled. Although the pub was lit up we soon found it had already closed. No amount of knocking produced a response. I considered offering my house as shelter, as it was nearest, but having come this far nobody was in the mood to end the night, or to spend half an hour walking back. Without any real agreement we clumped to the edge of the airfield. The wire fence was so thick with snow that the land beyond it was hidden, but, as we passed through, the space opened up. It was similar to the feeling you get at takeoff, when the falling landscape becomes massive as it moves away from you.

Only the hangar was unchanged, black and stark, but everything else was white. Even the ocean was white from spreading moonlight. Beyond the chalk lawn of the airfield we could see the Lake District, snow unbroken on the mountains. At that distance it was no longer white, but the exact same blue as a clear sky. The moon was glaring full, the few clouds that remained were cumulus, the sort you'd see on a hot day. Back-lit by the moon, their edges were bright and sharp.

We walked towards the clubhouse without speaking, but then carried on, Nicola saying she'd take us to see her aeroplanes – the Tomahawk and the Cherokee. Both were tied down outside and would be snowed over. It wasn't a long walk, or tiring, but after a while Katie and Patrick began to drop back. They made some drunken attempt to throw snow at each other, but it wasn't sticking and just flurried before it made contact. They dropped further back until I was left walking with Nicola.

'I think they're heading back,' she said. 'Should we keep going?'

'They'll probably just stay at the clubhouse.'

We continued, finding it difficult to speak, because Patrick and Katie had made it feel like we were pairing off.

We agreed to find somewhere to rest. The cold and the effort of walking in snow had combined with the booze to make us weary, but we didn't want to sleep.

We made it as far as the Cherokee and let ourselves in. Aeroplanes are never locked, only latched, and it was warm in there, the snow acting as insulation. We'd managed to get in without shaking the snow from the door, which meant it was too dark to see anything; the only light came where the snow was mottled. It was quiet enough for us to hear the click and scrape of the windsock as the breeze changed direction. We debated trying to get into the control tower, or even the shack for the flying school, but there was enough room for us to feel comfortable and we never followed up those plans. We whispered, because it was so quiet in there, and our voices were amplified back at us.

There aren't many other details that I can recall, but we talked until it came light, when wind blew rain on to the windscreen. As the snow washed away we saw clouds that looked darker than the sky had done at night. The airfield greened, its wet grass looking colder than it had when frozen. Tired, with headaches coming on, we agreed to sleep, but with no way to make the seats go back I think we both just sat there for hours, listening to the waves of rain shattering on the wings.

3 Ichor

Weeks later, in February, Patrick would drive down to the airfield and wander around on his own. At first I thought he was treating the location as though it mattered more than what had happened there. After a while, though, I realised he was going down there whenever it snowed, and usually at night. He'd park at the Crown and walk in, re-creating that night in as many details as possible. It was as though by creating similar conditions he might recapture the feeling of what had happened. I even caught him checking a calendar for full moons, trying to work out when the combination might be the same again.

As I pointed out to him, his efforts bordered on a certain brand of occult ritual. That type of working is all about creating moods and atmosphere, for an end result. If a specific set of conditions is met, you can create a mood and atmosphere that make you feel your end result has already been achieved. In doing so, you enable that reality to manifest. It's the sort of occult nonsense that fills the shelves of the New Age section, but which rarely works because it tends to reinforce doubts rather than create the required mood. The problem is that, for most people, rituals simply remind them of what they're striving for, underlining what they don't have. By working at them so hard, they actually reinforce what's missing, and keep things the same. It's often said that with ritual you get exactly what you ask for, and by working with fear people simply maintain their stagnation. We'd never bothered with ritual, or trying to create futures, because it seemed puerile and a bit unrealistic.

Despite this, I think Patrick was surprised when I pointed out to him that his airfield visits were a form of casual ritual.

'Jesus, Marcus, I'm being nostalgic, that's all.'

Usually, he'd never admit to any sense of nostalgia, so it was obvious I'd made a point. He also said that because snow was so rare along the coast he wanted to take advantage of the fierce winter. We were driving up the coast at the time, on a day that was a glare of low, dry sunshine. He went quiet for a while then said, 'And besides, I have trouble working out why that night bothered me so much.'

Having been there, I had some insight into why the night had affected him, even though what followed after we'd parted was relatively unremarkable.

After they'd dropped back from us, Patrick and Katie went to the clubhouse, both so drunk that they gave up on talking and slept on the floor, with nothing to cover them. They woke before it came light, their faces somehow next to each other. He found it difficult to breathe, because it felt as though she was stealing his air. When they kissed, he could taste beer in both their mouths. It was brief, and then he held her, neither of them speaking. Sometimes she would hug him, but then she'd move away, and with the easing of pressure he could feel the shape of her breasts against his chest. Barely moving, he spent the next few hours obtaining the smallest forms of contact – touching the cuff of her jumper, breathing in her hair, or lowering his palm on her ribs. She slept, motionless throughout.

When she finally turned away from him, Patrick rose and went to the window. Wind blew rain against the glass, and colour was returning outside, even the mountains being washed free of snow. There would be floods up there, he thought. He could see the Cherokee, one slash of red in the green-grey landscape. His gaze kept returning to the plane, although he had no idea we were in there at the time.

The drizzle on the glass made it too difficult to focus outside, so he sat on the floor, leaning against the wall, and watched Katie. Her body and neck were stretched, but she was still. There was cold air from the window, seemingly made cooler by the weak morning light. In sleep, Katie's face moved, possibly smiling, but although she looked warm there was a blue cast to her skin from the rainy air.

What had happened between them bordered on insignificance in terms of physical content, but Patrick was baffled by his emotions. He couldn't bear the thought of her waking up and leaving.

By the time Nicola and I arrived at the clubhouse, the light had changed, because the clouds had lost their glow. The air was browner, like river water, which would have suggested storms except that the temperature was dropping. It was the first thing I said to Patrick, something about the weather being unsettled. He couldn't even answer, but put a finger to his lips, because Katie was still sleeping. It disturbed me to see her in the centre of the room, where we always performed the rage. She was lying exactly where the victim would normally be. Although there would have been no residue there, it bothered me that she'd found that spot, and I was reminded of the reason that we'd initially been attracted to her. Whether this was lost on Patrick, I couldn't tell, but even as we went in, the sound of the wind and rain disturbed her, and she sat up, with no look of sleep or weariness. It made me wonder if she'd been lying there awake, waiting for Patrick to leave.

It was later than we'd realised, which explained our hunger. With no car, we walked silently in the rain. As it grew colder, the rain thickened and slowed, becoming snow again. Even on the wet ground it managed to stick.

When we got closer to the edge of the airfield, Patrick said we should eat something and suggested going to a café for breakfast. There were a few mute sounds of disapproval, of wanting to get home and have showers, but he persisted until we agreed. Patrick had left his car at my house, so from there he drove us to a café on the coast road, just a few minutes from the Lucas garage. We ate loads, and talked about flying, mostly, but Katie remained quiet. She refused to make eye contact with Patrick, but you could see that all his movements and conversation were based around glancing at her. Nicola and I would have left them alone, except that Katie made it clear from her mood that she didn't want that.

The light was all white outside, air moving snow, wind deepening. Although none of us acknowledged it, all four were acutely aware that she wanted to go home, he wanted her to stay.

It was Katie's lack of desire, I suggested weeks later, that had made him so keen. If she'd been friendly and warm, he'd have been as casual as ever.

'No, you misunderstand,' he said. 'I was already gone.'

Whatever else, I didn't want to lose track of Katie, given that she could contribute to our activities. It was difficult to see anything from her point of view now (perhaps because of Patrick's attention), but I had no doubt she could still be involved. I hoped to bring her into the process before spring, but Patrick put an end to that.

He only saw her once more, a week after that night at the airfield. Despite a phone conversation in which she'd said they could only be friends, he'd gone to the pub an hour early, full of hope. Where he'd normally sit back and listen, he talked. He didn't reveal anything about the rage or question her insights, but enthused about life and in particular flying.

While they talked, Katie's hands strayed to the objects near her, toying with a red paper napkin, shifting the ashtray. She didn't look at the objects, because her eyes were mostly on Patrick's. If she looked away, it was because she was thinking, or trying to picture what he'd described.

'What's it like, flying?'

'It's a relief for somebody to ask what it *feels* like. Most people ask how much it costs.' She looked happy at that, the sort of modest smile people have when you laugh at a joke they've told. 'Have you ever had a flying dream?' he asked.

'Once.'

'Then you know what it feels like.'

Before he could elaborate, she said, 'Don't you feel guilty, though, given the poverty that's around you? You're up there having a good time looking down on all this misery.'

'It's partly that perspective that I like. People down

here can be in a fury about something trivial, like where to park, but from up there it looks so insignificant. The distance does you good.'

'But not everybody can afford to get that perspective.'

'Flying is relatively cheap,' he countered. 'It's paying interest that makes people poor. And sometimes I'll choose to go a week without putting the heating on if I have to, so I can go flying. I don't feel guilty, but privileged.' He was flagging a little, because it was the last thing he'd expected from Katie, but he tried to inspire her rather than argue. 'I don't have a TV that works, but most people in this town do. My car isn't much to look at, either. I don't have much money, but what I do have I use well. My privilege is that I don't feel the poverty. I don't consider myself poor if I have the time to read and walk and eat. Real poverty is when you're so attached to stuff that you miss it when it's gone.'

At first he'd quite enjoyed her asking all the questions, but now it felt like an inquisition. He was uncomfortable with the line of argument he'd been forced into, because the real poverty that some people went through disgusted him, and he didn't want to deny their experience.

'I'm not saying poverty here is acceptable. It stinks. But the middle-class security most people are seeking would only drive them mad. They plot out a life with no surprises and then die of boredom.'

'So you never worry about where the money's coming from?'

'Never. Something always turns up.'

'That's OK when it's just you, but if you had a family.'

'I don't have, yet. But having a family doesn't mean resorting to fear.'

'But your partner would need some security.'

'People who *seek* security are the least secure of all,' he said. 'They insure everything, and live in constant fear of losing what they have. That's not security. When you're willing to let go, you have complete security, because it doesn't matter what happens.'

'So if you lost everything?'

'I'd just start again.'

He was confused, and found himself angry with Katie, but didn't want to show it. Her argument reminded him of people who whined on about the cost of space travel or firework displays while happily filling their houses with ornaments and televisions. It was the worst kind of small-minded hypocrisy, and he'd expected more from her.

They managed to talk about more neutral subjects after that, staying there until closing time. He'd made a vow years before never to push a night beyond its natural life span, but even as he walked her home he tried talking her into going somewhere else.

'I should have stopped trying to impress her,' he said after the event, 'and just told her how I felt.'

He'd impressed her more than he'd realised with his talk of adventure versus security. Primed for change, she'd acted quickly, giving up the lease on her flat and moving out within the week. The first we heard of it was when she sent Patrick a postcard from London, thanking him for the inspiration. What she'd gone there for, we had no idea, but our hopes of bringing her into the fold were gone.

The speed with which Patrick adapted surprised me. As soon as I'd accused him of fixating on the airfield, he stopped going back there and seemed to improve. We went there together a few times for the rage, and to work on the glider in preparation for spring, but he wouldn't even mention Katie. The only sign that he might be suffering was his desire to go out most nights.

Walking into town one Saturday evening, we hadn't planned anything in particular, so when we came out of an alley and found ourselves on John's road, I suggested going round. We hadn't seen him for weeks, and we knew he worried if we only ever met him for the rage. Patrick agreed, probably because we'd found our way there by pilotage.

After we'd knocked we saw a curtain pulled back, revealing the shine of his glasses and the stubble on his head. It took another two minutes for him to get to the door. From the outside his road looked like the best in town, with tall red-brick mansion houses, but inside the buildings had been sectioned off into cheap rooms, connected by white corridors that reeked of ash. John wanted to go straight out and tried to make us wait on the doorstep for him, but Patrick told him to fuck off and stepped inside. Although he barely took an interest in John, I knew his flat fascinated Patrick. It was smaller than most bedrooms, with a cooking area in the corner, which smelled of cold fat. The ceiling bulb had blown weeks before, so John was using the glow of the TV tuned to static, and one angle-poise. He lit a few candles, probably because he had guests, and motioned for us to sit on the bed.

He used the opportunity to get changed, swapping one oatmeal jumper for a slightly newer one, rummaging around the room for spare change. We just sat there watching, while he complained about the conditions he was living in. John never stopped complaining about how difficult it was to heat his room. The truth was that he never put the heat on, but when Patrick accused him of being stingy with the gas, he'd tap his chest, make a coughing noise, and say something like: 'It takes too much oxygen.' Whether that really bothered him or whether money was an issue was never made clear, but his flat was always freezing. A few days before Christmas I'd noticed him rubbing his little finger with his thumb, a chilblain spreading over the knuckle. His joints were swollen and grey now, his finger ends white, black and blue. Where his knuckles had split, he licked at the wounds. Coming out of the house we laughed, saying it was warmer outside than in.

John was unusually negative that night. He'd never been completely at ease with our activities, but I'd never known him complain about the state of his life. Whatever we talked about, he'd counter it with a criticism, not just of himself, but all of us.

'If we're so intuitive, if we're so in tune with the world,' he said, 'why are we stuck at the end of a thirty-mile cul-de-sac in Barrow-in-Furness?'

I'd never seen it that way, partly because of our responsibility, and also because there was a beauty in the town, if you knew how to look. Simply leaving or forcing more money into our lives would be an avoidance tactic. I'm not one to say that you have to accept your lot in life, but nor do I believe in hiding behind a mass of surface changes.

When we got into the pub, John went in first and I managed to make eye contact with Patrick, raising my eyebrows. Normally, he'd do the same back, but he furrowed his brow and shook his head. I couldn't tell what the expression meant, but then he said, 'We should get him a drink. Cheer him up.'

The alcohol worked, keeping John relatively calm, and we managed to keep him off the subject for an hour or so. It took a great effort, and we found ourselves talking about things that didn't remotely interest us to keep him occupied. We even tried to talk him into flying, because we knew he never would.

As closing time approached, John went quiet and I thought he was probably just drunk, but he kept looking out of the corner of his eye across the room. He wouldn't turn his head in that direction, but kept looking out towards the window. Patrick and I made eye contact again, but Patrick shook his head, presumably meaning we shouldn't humour him.

John pointed over to the alcove, where cushioned benches were built into the wall beneath the bay window. I could see two small tables, beer mats and ashtrays, but nothing unusual.

'Why do you think nobody's sitting there?' he asked. When we didn't answer he said, 'Nobody's sat there all night.'

'I don't know,' I said, wanting to appear nonchalant but feeling quite worried. It was akin to the feeling you get when somebody says they've heard voices in the house. It doesn't matter that you haven't, because you pick up on their fear.

'Can you see something?' Patrick asked.

'I'm not sure.' John sucked on his knuckle, examined the sores on his hands. 'What do you think?'

Something was different over there. I moved towards the space, holding my drink, pretending to look out of the window. Before I got near, I felt uneasy and didn't want to go any closer.

I shrugged at Patrick and signalled to Ian behind the

bar. He looked confused, so I curled my fingers, urging him to come over. Still gripping a Guinness towel, he walked over, keeping his distance. John and Patrick stared at the space rather than at Ian and myself.

'Did something happen here last night?' I asked.

'Nothing exciting,' Ian said, 'apart from a brawl with the police, but that was outside.'

'No arguments, somebody crying?' I pointed to the alcove as I said this, but Ian wouldn't look over. 'Was anybody sitting there alone?'

'Nobody. That I can remember.'

I wouldn't usually try to observe the pain in public, but Ian's reluctance was frustrating me, so I softened my eyes. It's much more difficult to do this when people are around, but I managed to see something in the corner, a glossy shape. The wire of pain was minute at its base, growing thicker as it rose, spreading like a glass lily coated in oil. In the artificial light it was almost impossible to see, despite its size, but the glimpses I caught shocked me. I'd never seen pain so wide and detailed.

'Something happened there,' I assured him. Now that I knew where it was, I could see it more clearly even while I was talking. This was a worry, because it's almost impossible to see the threads in artificial light unless they are fresh. Either the pain had been released within the last few minutes, or it was caused by extreme anguish.

'It could have been earlier tonight, even this afternoon,' I said.

Ian moved his hand around his face, rubbing his beard.

'I really can't remember anything,' he said, pulling the longer hairs with his fingertips. The other hand gripped his bar towel tighter. 'I'd better serve,' he said. 'Mum's visiting Dad again. In hospital.' He said the last part with a pathetic softness, as though I should feel sorry for him and stop pressing the matter.

I told the others I was going to attempt to take the thread in. John didn't move but looked concerned, so I said, 'We can't leave that much damage.'

Unattended, pain like that can grow. If people moved into its space, they would weaken. Their sadness would fill the thread, helping it to spread. That's why we tried to keep some parts of town completely clean; each was a refuge. Other places, such as the darker pubs near the Larches, or the car parks and alleys behind the Fraser Shopping Centre, were webbed with such established anger we were unable to take it in. By clearing our selected areas regularly, we maintained their purity and a sense of stability.

'If you're happy to look after it, that's fine with me,' Patrick said.

His confidence broke mine. 'Do you think we should ask Don first?'

Donald was the next victim, and if I took in the distortion, he was the one who would have to deal with it eventually.

'No need,' Patrick said, as though the thought of seeing Don cope with the pain was of perverse interest to him.

'Try to make sure nobody disturbs me then.'

I could have waited until morning, because the chance of the distortion being enlarged beyond repair during one evening was slim. Whatever happened in the pub that night, I'd still be able to cope with it. My eagerness was more to do with curiosity than need. There was something about the pain that bothered me, so I approached it, my chest and face in its direction, allowing the edge to spear into me. If I'd had any sense I'd have closed the wound at once, but I was tempted by its grandeur. Whatever had brought it into the world had to be of interest, and there was something familiar about its structure that made me want to read it.

It revealed nothing, making me feel numb and nervous, as though something was missing. It was like looking into a mirror and seeing myself standing ten feet further back.

There were people trying to get through to the seats. I couldn't hear their voices, but felt them pushing past. As the remains of the distortion slipped into me, I stumbled away, heading back to Patrick and John.

The hollowness of the thread had confused me. I didn't want to tell them, but it felt as though it had been put there deliberately.

A handful of times in your life, you might be walking around town aimlessly when you bump into somebody you haven't seen for ages, go for a coffee, then the pub, and end up in bed. Sometimes it even happens with people you've never met before, and whether you sleep with them or not, there's a momentum to the occasion that makes everything feel significant. The world seems to have blessed the two of you with the time, the weather and the mood to get along. Even though you don't stay together for long afterwards, there's a clarity to those meetings that you come to need. Sadly, such events occur more frequently in films than in the real world, but every time you leave the house alone you believe it could happen.

In recent weeks I'd spent quite a lot of time at the airfield, working on the glider but hoping to bump into Nicola. I didn't want to seek her out or pursue her, but hoped she'd be pleased to meet by chance, and find it inevitable that we should spend time together. I only saw her twice, from a distance, cycling away from the airfield. Even when I walked over to the flying school a couple of times, she'd either left or taken the day off. By April I realised that after three months of fantasising about seeing her again, something more constructive should be done.

That night in the Cherokee, Nicola had told me she'd been single for eighteen months, having left her boyfriend soon after she'd moved in with him. She'd quickly followed that up by saying she was going to spend a long time alone. I'd wanted to tell her that was the wrong thing to say. When somebody says they need to be alone, all you want to do is hold them and bring them back to warmth. You want to be the one who recovers their faith in love. As though reading my mind, she'd said, 'People think I need rescuing, but I don't.'

I've never been attracted to damaged people, to those who really need rescuing and looking after. John Gavaurin had this incredible knack of going out with women who'd been abused in one way or another, so he was convinced all women were bitter and unstable. At first I thought he was drawn to them in order to aid their recovery, but came to believe he was wallowing in the corona of their damage. Their pain never relented, and each one left him just a little more disillusioned than before. A few weeks later he'd find somebody else with a history of pain.

It wasn't like that with Nicola, because there was only the slightest hint of sadness in her voice. Rather than panicking about approaching thirty, single and insecure, she was happy that she hadn't married young or stayed in a shit job. Even so, I understood how she might feel, despite those convictions, because I was in a similar position myself. Although you know your situation is better than compromise, you sometimes feel intensely sad, but you can never admit it. If you voiced those feelings of loneliness – the logic goes – you'd end up married to some ugly bore within a fortnight. It's especially difficult when things are going well. When you've had a really good day and there's nobody to tell except your friends, it's quite frightening, but you can't acknowledge the fact.

I wasn't attracted to Nicola because she was sad but because she was being strong in the face of sadness. She didn't give in to loneliness or to fear about the future, but gained pleasure in the moment. She didn't need rescuing or to be told that she'd done the right thing, but I wanted to let her know how I felt. Even if she showed no interest in me, I wanted to show her that the way she felt about life made her pleasant to be around.

The next time I saw her came about because I was in town looking for Patrick. The lights had been off at his house, so I wandered around the more regular pubs, hoping to bump into him. The only place I avoided was the Lamb. Having taken in the swollen wound that week, I was brimming with disorder and reluctant to go back. Nobody else had reported finding similar fractures, but I remained anxious at the thought of returning. I knew that was the one place Patrick was most likely to be, but preferred to wander elsewhere.

It was cold outside, the wind bitten with rain, so that my face lost some of its expression to numbness. I stopped at each pub for a quick pint in an attempt to warm up, wondering when spring would become bearable. I'd just about given up and headed back down a road near the docks, lit only by a chill, steely reflection from the ships. There was no other light there apart from the glow of the hoarding at the Exchange, its halo flecked with sparks of rain. The door was heavy, and inside it was dark and hot, the air made slightly red by the heaters they'd switched on.

Nicola was sitting at the back, with three others, the table in front of them full to the edges with empty glasses. My hair and clothes were wet, eyes watering, and my face was slack with cold, so I considered going to the bar and pretending I hadn't seen them. Before I could, Nicola raised a hand, smiled, then pointed to her right. The person beside her, hunched over his drink, was Patrick. He gestured for me to go over to them, doing a better job than I was of looking unsurprised.

I didn't want to drink, but couldn't face joining them without one. Even as I headed over I knew that we'd all feel the need to explain why we were there. Patrick and I had made no arrangement, so he didn't need an excuse for being out, but there was something awkward about me stumbling across the two of them. I assumed this was the first time it had happened, and was relieved when Nicola confirmed my guess.

'I was out with Mark and Jo,' she said, indicating the couple who were with them. My arrival seemed to have sealed them off from the group, because they said hello then turned back to each other.

'And I just ended up here,' Patrick said. 'You know.'

'We've been talking about Katie,' Nicola said, and I couldn't help but smile. She'd said that as a way of affirming that she wasn't with Patrick as anything but a friend, and that helped put me at ease.

They talked about going out for something to eat, then laughed, because they'd been speculating about it for hours, resorting to crisps and peanuts rather than leaving.

They'd been drinking since late afternoon and couldn't be bothered to move on. The pub was so warm it made the unseasonable cold too difficult to take. When Mark and Jo shrugged their coats on, Nicola said she'd stay. There was a minute or so while nobody spoke as Jo and Mark left.

I hoped Nicola would go to the bar next, leaving me with Patrick, but he went for the next round, and although I was a bit pissed I agreed to have one more. Once he'd gone, it seemed like a good time to talk, and I felt I'd be able to be quite direct. There was too much noise, though, a group off to the right laughing louder than seemed necessary, and by the time Nicola and I had swapped the most basic details of what we'd been doing that day, Patrick came back.

He leaned in to tell her something, and she spoke back close to his ear. When she made eye contact with me, I smiled as well, pretending I'd heard, but I actually felt left out. They carried on talking, but rather than trying to join in I decided I'd had enough. I'd finish my drink and piss off if they were going to chat to each other all night. I knew Patrick would accuse me of being deaf, because I sometimes have difficulty in distinguishing words in crowded places, but that wasn't the point. They weren't making any effort to acknowledge that I was even there. It was possible the weight of pain I was carrying had encroached on my mood, but whatever the cause I didn't want to sit there feeling like I was in the way.

The pub was busy, especially in the section around the pool table. It was difficult to make out exactly what was going on there, because the cone of light over the pool table made everything else darker. Two angry-looking lads were trying to get a few games in, struggling to move the people around them out of the way. That isn't something you normally see, because when somebody's playing pool there's usually an arc of space around them. After all, the last person you want to annoy is somebody with a big stick in his hand. The people around them, though, were curiously quiet, but would then break into laughter. They all had a similar laugh, like a child being overexcited. At times it resembled a moan. Sometimes, when there was nothing on the jukebox, you could hear them breathing over the clink of the pool balls. I couldn't hear their voices, only their laugher. They kept putting their drinks down and gesturing at each other, the noises they made growing louder.

You could tell from the way they all rushed their drinks down that an agreement to leave had been made. It was only as they moved into the richer light by the bar that I realised they were deaf. They'd looked agitated because they'd had to put their drinks down each time they wanted to sign. Their laughter was loud because to them it was silent. In leaving, they made more noise, scraping chairs and laughing, sometimes saying sorry to people as they passed. More than anything, their voices reminded me of people pretending to be deaf.

The more frantic the noise and movement, the more Patrick struggled to speak. He was trying to get something across, but was leaning in towards Nicola. I could barely hear him but could tell he was talking about that night at the airfield again. I managed to catch the words: '. . . just wish things had worked out differently with us.'

Nicola looked at me, and I made no effort to hide my annoyance. I was about to slam my pint down and leave when Patrick's glass broke in his hand. It didn't shatter, but splintered, his hands resting between the long blades, bloodless, as his beer pooled across the table. It gave him the opportunity to make an issue out of how drunk he was, covering up for what he'd said. I quietly called him a dickhead, the sort of comment that wouldn't normally register, but which must have sounded bitter. More than anything, I was amazed his hand was unhurt, resting in so much glass.

On the following Wednesday I made my way home from work, ignoring the taunts of schoolchildren and the flickers of rain. The downpour had found its pace hours earlier and continued at that level, pulling crisp packets and grass down the road until they clotted in the mouths of drains. Puddles opened out on the road and filmed over with sunset, so it seemed like there was more light on the ground than in the sky.

With so little time before the rage I didn't want to eat, but couldn't bring myself to do anything but wait. Feeling swollen with the distortion I'd picked up at the Lamb, and pissed off at the way things had gone with Patrick, I sat in my armchair and looked out of the window, wondering what to say when he arrived. We hadn't spoken since that night out with Nicola, apart from a brief call when he'd said he'd pick me up. He came round with just a few minutes to go, so that we had to drive down the island more quickly than I liked. The sense of urgency meant we didn't even broach the subject of what had happened. The headlights made the rain dazzle like snow, making it difficult to see. The roads were so narrow that every corner was blind, and anything faster than ten miles an hour was a risk. If we were late, the others would just have to wait.

Something we'd learned a long time ago was that

cowering from the rain doesn't prevent you from getting wet; it only makes you look defeated. The angular, frantic movements people make when darting into a building save them only about two seconds. We preferred to risk a little water to maintain our calm. I followed Patrick into the clubhouse, where the other ten were already seated, water dripping from their hair, wetting the floorboards. It was quiet, and I was glad we hadn't barged in, charging away from the cold. With the door closed I felt the silence coming on and slowed my breathing.

Donald moved to the centre of the circle as we took our places.

On the opposite side of the circle, John's eyes narrowed in concentration. I knew the others less well, but we all made eye contact. It was a necessary part of our procedure, but the part I liked least, because in that condition expressions change. There's almost no personality left in the face, only the pressure of stored trauma. It was like looking at people in a coma, because their eyes were wide, the whites stark in shadowed faces.

As soon as Donald lowered his head, the stored pain came out of me. The release was almost involuntary, and I felt my breath stutter, rattling with a groan as the sound in the room returned. The hollow distortion I'd picked up at the Lamb was nosing out, visible as a dampening of light. It moved towards Don then passed into his face. He had the expression of somebody who has been spat at, the corners of white mouth dewy with sweat.

The others had emptied themselves into him, but the pain within me was still being expunged. The main bulge of it strained against my chest, then eased out and was drawn into him. Closure would usually come quite gradually, with the threads moving in as slowly as smoke, but they snapped from me and rushed into him. He moaned, stumbling to his knees, and I found it difficult to see, because the pain was damaging what little light there was in the room. Donald fell forward on to his hands, head drawn back. With a painful, yawning sound, a cough of watered food splattered from his mouth. I could feel the others tensing as we waited for him to soften the pain, but he knelt there gasping, staring at the circle of vomit. Another lurch widened it, coating his hands.

I'd never heard Donald scream, and because he had a low, gritty voice I didn't expect to hear such a high-pitched sound come from him. When he stopped, he appeared to shrink, curling in towards himself. It was dark now, making everybody faceless. After a deep breath Donald leaned further down on his elbows. The release came off his body and I closed my eyes with relief.

Don's reaction was something we'd avoided talking about that night. When the others had left the clubhouse, I'd remained behind with Patrick to wipe up the mess. Using only a couple of rags and water from the outside tap, it had taken longer than we'd expected. That had given us plenty of opportunity to talk about it, but we'd chosen not to. There was no stain from his vomit, but the scrubbed area shone obviously.

Three days later I went for a night in town with Patrick. John Gavaurin appeared from behind a wall at the library, as though he'd been waiting there for us, and tagged along once he knew we were going for a drink. As soon as we got to the Lamb he went for the first of his frequent urinations, and Patrick gave me a sour look.

'It's been a long time since we've had the chance to talk. Something always happens,' he said. Although that wasn't entirely true, I appreciated his desire to make a connection with me. 'But anyway, we'll be flying again soon.'

He gave me extra money for a double to down with his pint, and I went to the bar. There was no sign of Ian, only the casual staff, which made it take longer than usual for me to get served. John didn't return, which was his way of making sure I paid for the round, so I bought him a half. He reappeared as I set the glasses on the table.

If we couldn't bring ourselves to talk about Nicola in front of John, I'd have liked to talk about the impending flying season. We could bring the glider out of the hangar at this time of year, except for the changeable conditions. The weather was frequently safe, but less than stable, and we didn't want to keep letting the students down every time a cold front came in. It was better to wait for a period of predictable weather, so they could relax into being at the airfield.

We didn't get to talk about that, though, because John was already eyeing the space by the window alcove, where I'd picked up that hollow distortion.

'Do you think it was that thing that hurt Don?'

'I almost thought it was me,' Patrick said. It was unlike him to humour John at all, so I was surprised when he elaborated. 'I'd had a fucked week, I'd barely collected anything, but so much came out of me. I almost felt like I was putting my own pain into Don.' He said the word 'pain' with embarrassment. It was a word we used frequently to describe the emotional discharge of others, but seemed indulgent when talking about ourselves.

I doubted that Patrick had been the cause. Some of those involved in the rage thought our own pain was purified in the process, but I disagreed. Although Patrick's mood may have shaped his own experience, it was unlikely to have harmed Don.

I explained this and said, 'Otherwise, think of the effect John would keep having on the victim.'

'You have a point.'

John drank quickly, then said, 'Did you tell Don about what you'd collected?'

'We haven't told anybody, John. It's not unheard of for the victim to be consumed, so it might have been nothing.'

None of us believed that, especially as Don was usually capable of taking anything, but it was better to leave it like that. I didn't want to begin a startled speculation as to what might have created the distortion.

'If we find any more like that, we can begin to worry, but for now I'd just let it go.'

It was a weary night, and we went home early. The evening had been uncomfortable for many reasons, but I think the imminence of spring was getting to me. I was feeling the need to stop wasting my time in booze and become airborne again, even if it meant taking a risk.

There's something appealing about flying without an engine that goes way beyond the fear of death. People sometimes assume that if you fly you also go parachuting, white-water rafting and bungee jumping for the so-called thrill. Everybody who flies is slightly afraid of what they're doing, but fear isn't the reason we go up there. Although most flying stories concern freak storms, violent turbulence and mechanical emergencies survived, those aspects are little more than bravado. We talk about them because they're easy to describe and imagine, a way of getting across something of the flying experience. The reality of flight is much more difficult to communicate.

I think the reason people are drawn to flight is because it's an immediate form of meditation. This is what fliers mean when they talk about freedom; it isn't escapism, but freedom from the frantic mind. When faced with the vast space of air and the shimmering earth, your mind is emptied of clutter. It's impossible to be among the massive architecture of clouds, the horizon collapsing into bright rain, without being absorbed in the moment. You see everything but focus on nothing specific. Every movement and every shift in the air are felt, but you don't chase those sensations.

Most of the New Age crap that I sold at the Arcadia was filled with techniques and systems that were supposed to achieve such states of mind. We'd found that no technique was required, apart from being open to the sensations. Meditation isn't about being in a vacuum of trance but about expanding awareness. If you take the time to notice what's going on, to care about the quality of light, there isn't as much room for resentment in your life. We'd always found that by enjoying whatever we were up to, by absorbing ourselves in it, we weren't concerned with the things we couldn't change. Rather than concentrating on what was lacking, we enjoyed whatever we were involved with, no matter how simple.

If we made any mistake, it was to associate this sensation most strongly with flying. Although we'd enter winter enjoying the cold and the light, after months of ice we would withdraw and winter would pass with a sense of angst. We'd formed a habit of drinking our way through to the next flying season. If it wasn't for the cold flightless months, I don't think we'd have drunk at all.

During summer, if the weather relented, we'd be sober for months at a time. When you're sitting by the ocean, with the mountains of the Lake District on the north horizon catching the sunset, you don't need anything but the moment.

The flying students would sometimes ask us how we found the time and the money, and you could tell they were on the verge of giving up. You didn't have to give an answer, because they'd soon start telling you why life was too difficult and expensive, the irony being that these were middle-class people. The ones who stayed on for the whole summer were often unemployed or working in the shittest jobs.

Having sold so many crap books on motivation, I'd sometimes thought of writing a book called *Don't Wait to Fly*, aimed at those people who think it's beyond their means. I'd find it sad when I met people who asked about flying, and would then tell me how lucky I was, because they'd find it impossible to come up with the time or the money, even though their wages were five times mine. I'd respond by saying that gliding is almost free, and that if you stop watching television you'll find at least one extra day a week. You can't afford not to fly. But they wouldn't hear me, and would say, 'I've always wanted to fly, but I just can't afford it. Maybe when the guttering's finished . . . maybe when I've paid off the car . . . maybe when I'm dead.'

If you want to fly, all you have to do is turn up. When you get into an argument about that, though, you have to be careful how you phrase things. If you ever use a word such as 'providence' you'll be in trouble. 'How can you say the universe provides when millions of children are starving to death?' This is said in a tone that implies you're evil for doing something so indulgent with your weekend. This, of course, comes from the fuckers wearing Nike trainers which are sewn up in Third World factories in the hands of children. It's a difficult subject, though, because people assume you're summing up the whole of existence. That was never the case; it was just that in practical terms we'd found that if you refuse to struggle you get what you need, especially when it comes to flying. Of course, those who insisted that life was a battle also proved themselves right, and those who said they couldn't afford to fly never could. But more times than we could remember, we'd seen that when people did start flying, the money just turned up, rewarding their risk.

By the end of April, however, I was making my own excuses not to fly. I wanted to get up there, but was waiting for Patrick. Shenton was back in town, with his orange-fabric tow-plane, and the weather had eased. I should have got on with it myself, but the more difficult Patrick was about coming back to the airfield, the less I wanted to fly without him.

The delay lasted only about three weeks, but when I look back at that time it seems like an entire season. Patrick saw Nicola almost every day, but they spent most of their time in cafés and parks or at each other's houses. If they went to the airfield, it was to sit on its shore and talk rather than to fly. Sometimes he'd stay at her house, sleeping downstairs, so he didn't have to walk home.

If Nicola had fallen in love with Patrick, or if they'd had a one-off fling, I'd have found it easier to cope. It was the fact that they became good friends, and managed to maintain that friendship without me being around, that made me feel robbed. I couldn't work out how Patrick had managed to pull that off so effortlessly. If anybody should have been her friend, it was me, and Patrick should have spent at least six months getting over Katie. I was surprised at Nicola for being so taken with Patrick. Although I could understand the attraction (being his friend as well), it made me uneasy to think that in a straight choice somebody as interesting and original as Nicola had chosen Patrick. Worst of all, it was a definite choice, in that she'd become *his* friend, not *ours*. She only saw me when Patrick happened to invite me along.

There was an incident in the early stages that could have brought their friendship to an end. It was one of the rare days when the three of us went out together. On the phone, Patrick had made me promise not to pester him about flying. If I agreed to that, he said I was welcome to spend the day with them somewhere up the coast near Maryport. Having spent the previous week with John, or walking around on my own, I agreed eagerly. I even said he needn't worry about the flying. I'd probably just start the club up myself, before long, if he wasn't interested.

'This won't take for ever,' he said. 'I'll be back at the field by the time it's getting really warm. I think we'd be wasting our time if we start this early in the year. What's the point of being dragged up to three thousand only to glide straight back down? We should wait until the air's rising.'

I knew that was an excuse, covering for the time he was spending with Nicola, but I said, 'Whatever. I said I wouldn't bring it up, so you can let it drop.'

When I thought about this conversation, months later, I realised that his argument had distracted me from the most significant thing he'd said. *This won't take for ever.* Whatever was happening between himself and Nicola sounded like a plan, as though he was trying to achieve something through their contact. There was evidence of this on that same afternoon.

The weather looked rotten in the north, so Patrick drove east, then back around the southern mainland. He was trying to find an outcrop of land where the last wolf in England had supposedly been slain. He had no particular attachment to such an image, but it was somewhere to aim for, and a good place to walk. It was unsignposted, but we used pilotage and a modicum of map-reading to navigate. No other cars were there, and few paths led up from the beach, but we made our way on to a finger of land, cliffed on either side. It was windy, the grass short and brittle despite the ground being damp. You could see Barrow in the distance, Walney showing as a slither of black against the glaring ocean. It was that glare, and the way we narrowed our eyes against the wind, that brought the pain into view.

Whether or not this was a suicide hot spot, it was certainly a place where people had suffered. The air was ribbed with pain, the threads so twined and crossed that it was like looking through tears. I blinked, to see normally again, and looked at Patrick.

We'd stopped walking and must have been obvious in our discomfort, because Nicola said, 'What's going on?' She seemed to think there was a private joke.

'Marcus?' Patrick asked, as though to imply I was the one who'd stopped walking. It was a clever way out, and fortunate I was able to think quickly.

'I think I've been here before,' I lied. 'Something happened here.'

'Something bad?' Nicola asked.

'Maybe you killed the wolf,' Patrick said.

Nicola seemed bored by this and walked ahead, moving straight through the webs of pain. It made us wince, because if she lingered there her mood could easily be tainted.

'It's a long way from home,' I said. We'd never agreed on a limit to our activities, and had no idea whether people covered other areas, but it had usually been the case that we'd worked close to Barrow.

'Think, though,' Patrick said, his voice almost humming, because he was whispering deeply. 'If this place is left like this, and some poor pre-suicidal teenager turns up . . . It's hardly going to be a place to cheer up.'

I nodded as Nicola turned around, and he said, 'I'll tell her you need some space.'

'Give me half an hour.'

He walked towards her, nodded to his left, and they walked away together. She didn't even look across at me.

Although I've gained many insights into Patrick's life, from the afterglow of rage, I've rarely looked at the events of those weeks. I can't say whether that's out of respect for his privacy or because I don't relish seeing his intimacy with Nicola. The only moments I've seen are from that afternoon on the headland. It wasn't a time that had nudged at my curiosity, but perhaps I chose to gather an impression of that afternoon because I'd lacked interest at the time.

They weren't gone for long, but before they were even out of sight, Patrick had decided to take a risk. Partly to cover for me, and also because it gave him an opportunity he hadn't dared to create, Patrick said that he'd wanted to be alone with her.

'Marcus is fine about it.'

'He knows?' Nicola asked. She couldn't have realised the effect those words had on Patrick. To him, she was saying, *'He knows about us? He knows we need to be alone? He knows?'*

'Knows what?' was all Patrick could manage, hoping she would be the one to say it.

'I don't know. That . . .'

The path they followed had led inland and was heading down one of the cliffs so steeply that Patrick didn't think it was safe to follow. He stopped, and as both were sharing the path, they were closer than usual. When he looked at Nicola, though, she didn't hold eye contact but looked into the distance, then at the tree where her hand rested on the mossy bark. Water came out from it, putting sparkles on her fingers.

'I don't know if you remember that time in the Exchange,' he said, and she nodded so quickly it must have been clear what he was getting at. 'I wanted to say more. I didn't know whether you'd ever want.'

'You're a very good friend,' she said sadly.

Patrick laughed. It was involuntary, and in contradiction to his feelings, so he said, 'I can't believe I ever thought. I mean, I thought you might want to. So I thought it was better to be aired.'

'It is. I'm glad we've cleared it up.'

They stood there for a long time, and because she didn't change the subject or move on, he wondered if he should pursue it further. Perhaps she was being resistant, because she wanted to make sure he meant it. She turned around and shrugged at him, so he said, 'We should get back to Marcus.'

'He probably thinks you've got me up against a tree or something.'

At first Patrick laughed, glad that she could be crude. Joking about it was probably better than avoiding it, but then he felt winded, as though punched in slow motion. She'd clarified an image for him. He saw the two of them against the tree, and he was kissing her neck, knickers around her ankles, naked skin chilled by wind, his hands hot in her cunt, more aware of her hair and damp than he ever would be in bed. It was clearer than imagination, because her smell and skin mingled with bark and earth, the breeze moving in time with her breathing. Her words had made this image clearer than Patrick had ever fantasised, but at the same time assured him that it would never happen. As they walked back, he felt heady, perhaps from the exertion of climbing uphill, but also from his growing anger. The image was so potent it confused him, and a few times he even rubbed his fingertips to see if they were moist. He knew it hadn't happened, but it felt as though it should have done.

At the time, I was completely unaware of this, busied with collecting. The pain was largely unremarkable, but that might have been because I was forced to take it in so quickly. With no time to linger on the details, or even to make out the images, it all felt the same. When it was over, I felt a disturbing sense of melancholy. It's rare to feel anything when you're gathering pain, so to have been infected by the mood made me wonder if I'd done something wrong. Perhaps I'd been standing among uncollected pain, while harvesting the rest, and it had lowered my mood. As Patrick drove us back, I was slightly disturbed to recognise that I was actually enjoying the sensation. Maybe that's the definition for melancholy: pain that we enjoy hanging on to. Rather than dulling the senses like depression, it had enlivened me. I even enjoyed the fact that Patrick and Nicola had been alone, taking pleasure in the feeling of disturbance and mild jealousy. They were silent on the drive back, giving me time to wallow in the feelings. It was past sunset as we drove into town, the orange lights of the coast road set in a bright blue twilight; there was nothing else to see, no other colours or shapes. I was overwhelmed by that view, physically aching with the beauty. It was similar to the feeling when you're getting a cold; it's almost pleasant to feel your body giving in and needing a warm bed. There was no sense of misery, no need to drink or sleep, only the feeling that the night was gorgeous.

The first flight of the year came soon after. Patrick arrived at my house on time, but I could tell it had been an effort. I had no idea where he'd picked up a hangover, but it made him look colder than usual, and he squinted against the morning sun as he drove. I asked him if he was fit to fly, and he steered with one hand, holding the other out to show how steady it was.

'I feel like shit, though,' he said as we pulled on to the airfield.

Between the main gate and the clubhouse, there was a rarely used taxiway, but it was common courtesy and good field practice to stop and look both ways. That morning was the only time I saw him drive across without pausing. The light over the grass was pearlescent, the hawthorn hedges at the perimeter in full blossom. At that time of year, when the sun comes out, there is so much moisture on the flowers and grass that it comes into the air and shines. The humidity makes the atmosphere glossy, but although everything is hazy, it feels more real than when sharpened by winter.

Shenton was over by the tow-plane, his posture so shifty he looked like he was about to steal it. The students were gathered in a group by the hangar doors, and they stared as we drove to the infield.

I loved this part of flying as much as being in the air. A few people who start flying soon give up, because they imagine arriving at the airport, hopping in a plane, flying around, then going home and doing all this within the space of an hour. They quickly find that you need at least three hours to fly for one. The critics put this down to the checks and plans, but really it's because time slows down, gently, at an airfield. Why rush to fly, when you can sit on the grass and watch spot-landings for half an hour? For those who keep flying, the appeal is being around the aeroplanes, and the sense of space you get from a piece of land that allows flight.

'You don't want to shag somebody on the day you meet them,' was the way Patrick put it to the students that morning. Most of them were there for the first time, and, although one or two at most would carry on through the summer, Patrick briefed them as though they'd never give up. He thought it was important to stress the experience of flight as much as the details. Many of them had come armed with books and guidelines, expecting some sort of technical equation to be carried out via an aeroplane. Patrick made sure they felt flight before they thought about it too much. 'But don't be too eager to fly. This is a beautiful place and it's a beautiful activity that we're carrying on with, so don't wish your day away.'

'I can hardly believe I'm doing this,' one of the students said. 'This place is so close to town, but you never think of coming out here. It feels like we're hundreds of miles away.'

One reason I loved the airfield was that, although it was physically similar to any other piece of ground around Barrow, it was made different by the idea of being an airfield. It was the idea of flying that made it feel so far away.

It was cool and cloudy, but calm enough for us to fly, and as we wheeled the glider to the runway Patrick said I could take the first student.

'Just in case rats have eaten the wires,' he said.

I was methodical about the pre-flight checks, not only because the glider had been stashed away for so long, but because I enjoyed being near to it. Shenton's plane was ready on the centre line, ready to be hooked up, but I wasn't going to rush. While I did the walk-around, Patrick strapped the student into the front seat. Gary was about thirty, his head shaved to hide the onset of baldness, and he kept telling everybody this was his first flight. He didn't have any idea what to do.

The seats of the glider were warm with sunshine, and it was quiet in there. When the canopy is locked, you realise how much noise there is outside, even on a remote airfield. It was so quiet that the sound of our harnesses and the movement of our shirts and feet were amplified. I ran through the checks, making sure I had full and free movement in the controls.

I spoke to the tower briefly, Don replying formally, and they hooked us up to Shenton's plane on the centre line of runway two-four, heading across the width of the island to the edge of the sea.

'You all right?' I asked, and Gary nodded.

I gave Patrick the signal, and he waved Shenton off and ran with the wing until there was enough lift to take it from his hand. The hangar passed on our left, then the control tower, and as the rim of the sea tipped into view behind the grass banks I could feel the wheels go light. There was pressure in the controls, enough response to allow flight. I lifted us just before the tow-plane, then it climbed and we followed in formation. As we climbed the sea opened up, miles wide; at the shallowest point I could make out the fern-like flurries of sand discharged by streams. Turning inland, I looked down at the pre-fab estate, hundreds of poverty-line retirement homes, nothing more than pastel-painted caravans with roofs attached. One strong wind could clear the lot of them, I thought. We turned towards the town, and I orientated myself, noting the bulk of the sub-house and the coast road.

I warned Gary we were about to leave the tow-plane and pulled the cable release. Shenton dived to the right as we climbed to the left and the air became hushed. I levelled off, and told Gary to put his hands on the stick.

'You have control,' I said, which is always an irony when you're handing over to a first-time flier. 'Just be gentle, and keep it straight.'

By the time I'd shown him the effects of the controls and let him do a couple of turns, we had to head back, and I turned us on to the downwind leg. One thing I can never be accused of is being a distracted flier, but something was bothering me. It was my first landing of the season, but I felt concerned by something, and couldn't tell what. I fed the air brake in and out to adjust our glideslope, and the landing was better than it should have been, given my distraction.

'Do the first stint, if you like,' Patrick said as Gary got out.

You could tell that Gary wanted to enthuse but didn't

know who to talk to. While the next student strapped herself in, he started telling the others what it was like, never speaking to a particular person, just talking generally. It was Patrick's job to keep his enthusiasm up and to hint that he might get another flight so he wouldn't go home. The more people you have, the easier it is to keep things running smoothly.

The turnaround that day was so rapid I didn't get much chance to talk to Patrick. After the first run, Patrick took over and didn't get out for the rest of the day. He insisted on a working lunch, chomping a sandwich in the time it took for us to get the next student in place and hook everything up.

It was only when everybody had finished their second flight, in the early evening, that I realised why he'd been rushing.

'Same time tomorrow,' he said to the students, 'weather permitting. Just send us off, would you?' Then he gestured for me to join him. 'Come on, we've not been up together for years.'

One of the younger girls ran with the wing for us, and as we took off Patrick said, 'I thought we should have a look at the sunset from up here.' The sun was low enough to have lost its glare, but Shenton turned away from it earlier than normal. It was a while since I'd seen a sunset from the air, at least a year, and this one confounded me. As the tow-plane broke away, Patrick turned back towards the ocean. We flew towards the sun for no more than two minutes, but time slowed, and my hearing went dead. I couldn't sense any movement, even from the wings, and the frame around me was absent. It was the sort of paradox that occurs in dreams; it felt like a few seconds, but also like several hours, flying into the sun. The illusion was broken when the base of the sun met the water line. Where it touched the sea, the edge of light was pulled on to the water like surface tension. As Patrick turned on to base, I looked down at the pre-fabs, the sunset making them orange.

As we climbed out, the sun had gone and the town had turned the colour of twilight, lights coming on. As we wheeled the glider back, I could make out the Lucas garage. Distant figures were walking on the forecourt around cars, and the overhead lamps were switched on.

I was glad that Patrick hadn't spoken during the sunset, but the feeling that had bothered me on the first flight was disturbing me again. It was difficult to pin down, but I realised that being up in the air hadn't changed much. I'd been anticipating a moment in flight that would free me, put winter behind and help me cheer up. That sunset and the stillness should have been enough, but I was left feeling slightly angry.

It reminded me of the way John would put so many conditions on his happiness. 'If I just had a bit more money ... if I could meet somebody new ... if I didn't get ill so often.' He was always looking for external causes to blame his misery on, but as soon as they were cured his depression would find a new direction. In a similar way, I'd been accepting a mild depression, thinking that it would be cured by flying.

Patrick was silent, but sensing that he might speak I rushed through these thoughts, trying to work out what was wrong with me. I knew that something was missing but couldn't tell what.

Later that month I walked to the east of the island, partly for the sunset but also to be near to the Roundhouse.

Keeping away from the main door, I walked through the car park. Most of the spaces were taken, but I noticed a skinny, cold-looking man standing by his white Escort, smoking, urging his mongrel dog to do something. I couldn't tell what he was trying to persuade it to do, but each time it came back at him, circling to get closer, he pushed it away with his foot, pacing, smoking more, looking out to sea. Something about his posture bothered me.

I stayed closed to the restaurant, because being so high it afforded the best view. Below was the nearest thing to a beach you'll find anywhere near Barrow, a strip of gritty sand next to grass, just across the road from the main estate. If you stand with your back to the island on a clear day and ignore the rigs and ships, you could imagine you were somewhere foreign.

Curried fat steamed from the fans at the back of the restaurant. There were no windows to see in (all being curtained or painted over), so I had no way of telling whether Suzette was working. I hadn't seen her since she'd split up with Patrick, so she could have moved on to a new job months before. I knew where she lived, but turning up at her house would seem too direct. If things didn't go well out here, I could at least pretend I wanted something to eat.

I was nervous about going in, mostly because she'd been Patrick's girlfriend. I hadn't told him my intentions, but if anything happened I resolved that I would. He came round so rarely now, and had even cancelled a couple of weekends flying (leaving me to keep the students occupied all day), and I was getting sick of it. I refused to be part of a predictable love triangle, going out with him and Nicola while yearning for them both. I could never tell whether Patrick knew that I'd liked Nicola, or if she had any idea, but the faint suspicion that they might be laughing at me was too much. Even if it wasn't direct laughter, they might have been getting off on having me with them and sensing my need.

On one of the last times I'd been with Patrick, he'd been talking about Nicola, and I'd said, 'I wish you two would just fuck and get it over with.' He insisted that nothing was going on, but that was far from the truth. He enjoyed being with her, not just because they were friends but because the agony of longing for her was more pleasant close up than at a distance. It was even possible she was using Patrick for the emotional attention, always being wanted. These thoughts had been building, but hadn't become quite so bitter until my walk across the island. I think I was trying to justify the fact that I had every intention of sleeping with Suzette.

I wasn't trying to get back at Patrick, but Suzette was one of the few women I knew. I'd be able to talk to her without all the usual first questions, because she knew who I was. I didn't think there'd been any sexual tension between us when she was Patrick's girlfriend, but there would be no harm in seeing how we got along now.

I still hadn't plucked up enough courage to go in, when she came out of the door, heading for her car. I turned away, embarrassed, just catching a glance of her recognising me as she unlocked her car door.

'Marcus?'

I waved and went over, quickly thinking up a lie about being there for the sunset, even though it had gone dark.

'Do you want to go somewhere?'

'Sorry?'

'Do you need a lift?'

'No, I was just walking.'

She looked tired, but more pleased to see me than surprised. Her hair was longer, but still in a ponytail. She was wearing an old black leather jacket, the sort boys wear before they can afford a motorbike.

'I was just picking up my wages,' she said, tossing her bag on to the car seat. 'How's Patrick?' She undid her ponytail, scuffed her fingers through it, and tied it back up, all with her eyes closed, listening.

'Well enough, I think,' I said, surprised at how quickly she'd got on to the subject. 'He's not around as much, but yeah, he's OK. How are you?'

I couldn't tell whether the strain in our conversation was because we were talking about Patrick or because she guessed why I was there. We carried on talking, her standing behind her car door, me with my hands in my pockets. We were running out of things to say, so it was either going to be goodbye or somebody would have to suggest going on elsewhere. She'd already offered me a lift, but I wasn't heading anywhere except here.

She rubbed her arms then folded them, hunching to indicate cold, and said, 'Do you want to get in?'

Getting into a car for the first time, you notice the smell. Mostly it will be old seats and Magic Tree, but there are always distinctive musts, which make every car unique. There was old cigarette smoke here, but I could also smell Suzette, her leather jacket and a perfume I remembered from months before. It reminded me more of Patrick than her.

We didn't go anywhere for the first hour, assuming it was just going to be a brief chat out of the breeze. Before long, the windows had steamed up with our talking, but we were too close to look at each other the whole time.

Instead, we stared at the fogged windows, focusing beyond them as though we could see a horizon. She didn't talk about Patrick much, but everything she said was related to the aftermath of his leaving. She'd resisted going on antidepressants, unwilling to let a break-up define her life. Then, when she found she couldn't sleep without drinking, she'd tried Prozac. 'I just sat still, all day, you know, thinking I was all right. Coping. So I decided to come off it, but didn't wean myself away from it. I just stopped one morning. Big mistake. Head rushes, panic attacks. I started to think if I'd just never taken that poison I'd have been fine.'

'And now?'

'It doesn't matter how switched on you are,' she said obscurely. 'You think you know everything, and then . . .' Not understanding what she was saying, I stayed quiet, and after a deep breath she tried again. 'I mean, I thought I could cope, you know, if he left me. I have a life of my own. I don't depend on him for my happiness.'

'He said you weren't too upset.' I was trying to encourage her, but her face dropped.

'You think you're going to be all right, but then you're just not. Even now, I have moments when I could cry. Not *because* of him, but because of how I felt afterwards. I keep trying to be all right, but sometimes I feel like I'm just wasting away. That can't be because of one person, can it?'

'He's not that special,' I said, half-seriously.

She was sitting stiller than I'd ever seen her, so that most of her movement came from breathing.

'And it's not as though he even involved me in the stuff that made him special. The gliding, his obsessions.

All those hours he spent with you, messing about with things. I never got to know the person I sensed was there.'

I wanted to talk about that more, to say I felt the same, but she carried on. It was good, in a way, to hear her talk, because it kept me from brooding. She said she was trying to renew her life, keeping busy and reading more books.

'I'd even considered flying, because that's what people do when their lives feel empty.'

'Thanks.'

'No, but you must see that all the time – people looking for meaning.'

'Sometimes they find it,' I said. 'You should try it.'

'It would just mean I kept bumping into him.'

I was going to suggest other things she could do to meet more people and stay sane, but she countered that before I even spoke. The problem, she said, was that everything felt like a hobby, a pastime, some way of coping with what happened.

'You fill your life with stuff, because you can't bear to sit down and think. Instead of having a life, you keep busy so you can cope. I don't want to just cope.'

I'd no idea she'd been that much in love with him, but I knew if I even suggested that, she'd say it hadn't been love.

'And it's not just me,' she said. 'Everybody at our age has done this. You get into one big relationship in your early twenties, and you live with that for years, and then you both get restless and give up on it because you've never lived. Has that happened to you?'

'Well, sort of. I was fourteen, but it was similar.'

'And after that you just can't settle into anything. Even the word "settle" sounds unclean, so there's this urge to move on all the time. I think that's how it was with me and Patrick; we chucked away what we had towards the end because it seemed so boringly normal. You can't compromise, there's nothing worse. But that means you end up on your own.'

'You can't blame a person for what's missing in yourself,' I said, because her voice had started to catch, as though she might cry.

She seemed to relax, wiping a space in the breath on the windscreen. There was nothing to see but dark.

'People do matter,' she said. 'I know you have to be your own person, or whatever. But I'm sick of going home on my own all the time.'

When you feel like crying, but resist, the pain solidifies in your throat. If you just let go, and cry, that pain goes. It's the holding back that hurts. I felt sorry for her, not for what she'd said but for the way she'd said it. There was neither a plea in her voice nor a request for me to go back with her, but such a plain sadness. Having walked home alone so often, rained on and trying to stay upbeat, I knew exactly how she felt. You can keep telling yourself that everything's all right, but that sort of casual loneliness is almost unbearable. It's so mundane that it comes down to this: no matter what you do, being on your own is no good when it's against your choice. You know you can't admit to that, most of the time, but when somebody else allows you to, the pain surfaces.

I tried to swallow, the tension in my throat like a sharp stone. When I looked at Suzette, I thought there were tears in my eyes, but the diffusion was coming from her. Pain lifted from her body as though she was shedding dim light.

Even at that point I was filled with the expectation of seeing her naked. I wanted to get away from where we were parked, because we were probably contaminating the place.

'Do you want to go somewhere else?' Suzette asked. 'We can go back to mine, or go out or something. I could do with a drink.'

It was a freezing night, but she drove with the window down, so she could smoke. It's the smoke I remember more than anything from that night: in the pub at the end of her road, then as we walked back. It was in her room and clothes, and even on her skin. When we kissed, she was still exhaling, and she tasted stale and fresh at the same time, somehow organic.

I wasn't particularly drunk or tired, but it's only the smells that come back clearly. There are glimpses of her body – the shine of her skin in a room full of streetlight – but the details have gone.

Waking early, I couldn't emerge from a difficult dream-state. The room was blue, partly with morning but also because Suzette was smoking again. She blew from the side of her mouth, away from me, but the room had hazed. I wasn't sure where I was, and – unable to wake fully – I kept thinking the smoke was gas. I thought she ought to put that cigarette out or the whole room could go up.

I've always been awe-struck by characters in historical novels who wait years for the person they love. Sometimes they choose to be alone for ever, if that's what it takes. I like the idea of such sacrifice, but I'd want to be seen doing it. If nobody knew you were suffering, it would seem more sensible to move on and make the best of a bad time.

Once I'd slept with Suzette I felt envious of Patrick,

thinking that his patience with Nicola was remarkable. After a few days, it occurred to me that he had the advantage of being in her company all the time. It's easier to believe something will happen when you're around the person, especially if you're close. If I'd been able to spend those hours with her, I'd have found it pleasant to linger in the anticipation, gaining hope from the proximity. Seeing her so rarely, I'd given up.

The few times I had seen Nicola recently, I'd still winced, especially when I saw the calm delight on her face as she watched Patrick. If I didn't know the full story, I'd have thought she loved him. I wasn't enraged by it any more, just a bit jaded, and distressed that my feelings continued even though I'd stopped hoping. Being with Suzette hadn't changed anything, and I knew my feelings would probably remain for a while, no matter how many people I slept with.

For her part, Nicola worked to discourage Patrick by playing on his desires for Katie. She encouraged his memories, and built this mythology of him waiting for Katie to come back. He played up to that at times, to put her at ease, but then every few weeks he'd find himself unable to resist asking again. He felt she'd given signals that things were different, but each time she'd look surprised, then weary and anguished as she told him that nothing had changed.

She kept her distance until a Thursday in early August, when it was too windy for flying. They spent the day walking around the coast, near Millom, talking so much they lost track of where they were, ending up by a small lake they'd never heard of before. There were trees around the edge, and wild wheat so blanched it flared in the dull light. Nicola became quiet and walked ahead of him.

Patrick trailed her as she moved from place to place, surveying the surface, dipping her fingertips in the water, wiping them on her coat. Her back was to him the whole time. Clouds pulled apart around the sun, and when she stood next to him he was able to see her hair flickering against her neck. She looked past him, and he thought that if she made eye contact he'd tell her he loved her. She said something he didn't hear, then walked on, reluctant to look at him. The few times she did glance back, her expression had that furtive brevity you get when you keep making eye contact with a stranger.

On the way back they stopped at a pub, north of town, and she asked if he'd drive the rest of the way so she could drink. She led him to the quietest corner, and sat next to him against the wall. Patrick knew not to talk, and after a minute of silent drinking Nicola said, 'If it was anyone, it would be you.' It felt like they'd been having this conversation all day, with their gestures and thoughts, and this was merely a continuation.

He wanted to know if she had some history of being hurt, some reason for avoiding a relationship, but she said there was nothing.

'But you do like sex?'

'Yes, of course.'

To hear that, and to be sitting so close to her in warmth, was unbearable.

'So it's just that I'm too disgusting?' He tried to make light of it, but his words had an edge.

'It's just that I don't want that, at the moment, with anybody. I love you, but I don't want that.'

'So sex would spoil it?'

She reached under the table and held his hand. The

way she touched him felt more like the way you'd touch somebody in hospital than a caress.

'We never get angry, we never expect anything of each other. It's so beautiful to feel this close, without having arguments. It would be tragic if we ever bickered.'

'Sleeping with somebody doesn't mean you automatically treat each other like shit.'

'We might spoil our friendship for nothing.'

'The only reason our friendship is so flawless is because I'm waiting.'

'I don't believe that,' she said, her eyes closing.

'But we couldn't carry on like this if one of us had a girlfriend or boyfriend. This is a relationship whether you admit it or not. We're going out with each other, but we don't fuck.' She didn't respond, but let go of his hand. 'I'll fuck just about anybody,' Patrick said, 'because I enjoy it. Why won't you?' Given the hours he'd spent thinking of persuasions and explanations, and ways to communicate his certainty, he was startled to find how readily he'd attacked her. He'd imagined things going much more smoothly than this.

'It's better to have love than to be fucking without it,' Nicola said. 'And I'm not saying never. I don't intend to go my whole life like this. I love sex,' she whispered. 'I love it. But it's not fucking.'

'You think I want to just fuck you? You *know* how I feel.'

She leaned forward on her elbows, rubbing her eyes, then sat back.

'Maybe you're right. But all the arguments in the world don't change how I feel. And I don't want to.'

'It's very convenient, isn't it. You get to keep me, without any commitment.'

'You're so wrong. You know I'm not going anywhere.'

'So why try to be so pure? There's nothing spiritually advanced about frustrating yourself.'

'I don't want to sleep with you unless we're going to stay together.'

'That's the point, though,' Patrick said. 'It's not the sex that actually bothers me. It's that I want to be with you, rather than anybody else.'

'You already are.'

As they drove back they talked more generally, and his mood improved. Although he'd countered her comment at the time, he'd been stunned by her speculation that she might eventually want to be with him. She'd talked about staying with him as though it was a real possibility. Patrick had grown so accustomed to expecting failure that the thought of actually being with her was unfamiliar. It was easy to take joy in being near Nicola, but he wondered what would happen to his feelings if he could touch her whenever he wanted. He thought about the way he used to casually grope Suzette's breasts while she was cooking or talking. To become as casual about Nicola would be worse than never seeing her again.

If she'd changed her mind on that journey home, and invited him to bed, he wouldn't have known what to do with her. Despite all this talk of sex, all he really wanted to do was hold her.

Patrick tried to explain all this to John and myself. The three of us were out in the rain on a Sunday morning, checking for pain. There was a pub I'd never been to before, and John wanted to go there while it was quiet. Patrick was coming with us for the first time in weeks, and that was probably why he felt able to talk in front of

John. He knew he didn't get to see me often enough to wait until we were alone. The walk was longer than I'd have liked, given the weather, but it was good to spend time with the two of them again. John squinted into his glasses as we walked, trying to peer through the drops. Patrick talked without let-up, but he kept asking if we understood.

It was a wide street, inviting gusts of wind. Being on the edge of town, it opened towards the hills rather than other streets. Nobody was about. The only colour was a chalkboard outside the pub which read: *Sunday Strip, 12–1*.

'Did you know about this?' I asked. John shook his head, rereading the words, but Patrick didn't seem to have noticed. He was looking down the street.

'Sunday afternoon?' John said. From his confusion I guessed he hadn't known.

It was raining steadily, but the wind made it feel heavier, and I wanted to either get inside or head home.

'I suppose we can just warm up,' John said. 'We don't have to watch.'

It was cold in the pub, perhaps because it was so cavernous. It felt like a school hall that had been converted, but the tall windows had been blacked out to make it feel more like a pub. The few bulbs that were working lit only small pools of space. There was a stage next to the bar made from boxes, covered with black sheets, but there was no sign of the stripper. John headed for a seat off to one side – but still with a good view of the stage – leaving Patrick and me to get the drinks.

'There's almost nothing here,' he said quietly, which was surprising. Being a building we rarely ventured into, you'd think it would have been riddled with pain.

'Perhaps they're all just too pissed.'

We drank for a while, taking it in turns to go to the toilet or to move around the main room, recovering what we could. It's not easy taking in pain when people are watching, especially if their glares make you self-conscious. It was probably the need to be slow and careful that kept us in there, drinking, until the stripper came on stage.

She was wearing a cardigan over her sparkly top and carried a tape-player and a leather bag. I hadn't imagined a teenager coming out, but was surprised to see somebody who must have been close to fifty. I couldn't tell whether the excessive make-up was meant to be erotic or some sort of disguise.

'If we walk out now,' Patrick said quietly, 'we'll never be forgiven.'

I didn't feel as threatened as he implied I should have done, because there weren't many people to worry about. Closest to the stage was a lad of about twenty in a wheelchair. He had the blackest hair, and I kept staring at him to work out if it had been dyed. Other than that, there were a few old men, one couple, and single men drinking more than we were.

'We won't even be noticed,' I said.

'*She'll* notice. I couldn't do that to her.'

The stripper switched on her tape and began moving differently, looking at faces for the first time. With nothing to do at the bar, the landlord stopped to watch. The music was so quiet you could hear her breathing, the sound of her clothes coming off. She didn't take long to get naked, her shaven twat inky with a snake of tattoo. It was difficult not to look, but I tried to watch other people instead, to see how they reacted. Nobody was smiling or looking remotely turned on. I'd thought the lads might jeer or laugh, but they were silent. From their faces, you'd think they were undergoing some sort of punishment.

The one in the wheelchair was moving in time with the music, his body rocking from side to side. It must have been just his legs that were the problem.

The stripper pulled out a big green dildo from her bag, then some gel. She wet it, then pushed it in, pulling herself to the edge of the stage, so she was close to the wheelchair lad. She put her ankles on his shoulders and popped the dildo in and out of herself rapidly. With alarming speed the lad got his dick out, instantly wanking with a vigour that surprised me. She tried to stop him, closing her legs, telling him fiercely, 'No, love. No.'

He stopped, slumped, and the air around him fractured.

Everybody looked uneasy, but the three of us recoiled, seeing the spread of his pain.

'I really think we should go. Patrick? John?'

They stood, backing away with me, watching the warped area widen around him. The stripper carried on, standing again, dancing, raising her arms over her head. You could barely see her through the distortion.

Outside, the rain had thickened, but my face was so hot I welcomed the spray.

'We'll have to go back there for that, sooner or later,' John said. 'One of us will.'

'I just couldn't watch that any more.'

Patrick was quiet, but then suggested we get to a café. Somewhere had to be open on a Sunday lunchtime. We managed to find a place next to the bus station, which was more pleasant than we were used to. They'd gone to the effort of filling the place with dark wooden tables, and there were stained-glass windows. It was expensive, though, so virtually empty.

I was bothered by what we'd seen, not because his pain was so extreme, but because it occurred in a room where there were so few traces of damage. It made me wonder if we'd been missing something obvious. I think we'd have made more of the incident, except that before our coffees were even finished Patrick said, 'Fuck me. That was Katie Oswald.'

He was looking behind me, out of the main window, hesitating. Then he got up and moved quickly, leaving John and myself to wonder whether or not we were meant to follow him.

Flying goes well if you're not really trying. You have to concentrate and commit to the moment, but too much effort just gets in your way. This is never more obvious than with new students. The first time you let somebody try the aero-tow, they struggle at the controls like they're playing a video game, straining to keep things in place. As a result, the aeroplane bumps around more than if they were to relax their hold. This is also true in turbulence, where new fliers are tempted to correct every buffet and thud in the air. Partly this is from fear that the movement is dangerous. When you hit a ridge of turbulence, the last thing you want to do is bank the aircraft hard over, but that's exactly what you have to do, to stay in the rising air. Each time this happens, I take over and show them how easy it is to regain control by letting go of effort. If you stop trying to fight the movement, and let an aeroplane ride the air, it will almost fly itself.

Every student we'd ever taken up had fought the controls, with the exception of Katie Oswald. It was the thought of flying, she told Patrick that rainy lunchtime, that had brought her back to Barrow. 'And seeing your lifestyle. Despite this place, you're all happy. You're not pushing for anything.' She said that she'd felt stretched in London, busy filling her time with rush, and never feeling calm. 'I didn't feel like I could see properly.' She said that in the middle of a string of descriptions, but it was the one Patrick fixated on. It meant, perhaps, that her renewal would continue.

The number of students had halved in recent weeks, so Patrick told her to come down on the following Saturday. She rang him once before then, asking to talk it all through first, but he was seeing Nicola and didn't want to cancel. She promised to be there at the weekend.

When we arrived, the students were wheeling the glider out of the hangar, but Katie was outside the clubhouse, on tiptoes, looking in the window. She turned to smile at us when we pulled up. Patrick stopped the engine, then wiped at his face as though drying it with a towel and blinked overtly. He heaved air deep into his lungs, then got out of the car.

Usually, I liked his manner with students, because he managed to generate a sense of excitement; you could tell that whatever else was bothering him, he never tired of flying. That's why it surprised me to see him being so quiet with Katie. After she'd made eye contact with me, I could tell she was trying to do the same to Patrick, without success. He looked across at the windsock.

'I was going to risk soloing Gary today, but not if it's gusting like this.'

For Katie's benefit I said, 'The crosswind can be enough to tilt you over when you're landing,' miming the action with my hand. 'You have to bank into the wind to stay on track.'

We were forced to use runway two-four, regardless of the wind direction, I explained, because Donald sometimes insisted on keeping the main runway free for powered fliers. There had been perfectly clear days when we'd been grounded courtesy of this ruling, even when the main runway was scarcely in use, because the crosswind on two-four was so severe.

Patrick said, 'I'll get down to the others,' and handed me the clubhouse keys. I went into the clubhouse to get an insurance form for Katie, and she followed me in. On a Saturday morning the clubhouse felt like a completely different place from the room we use for the rage, but there was a chance Katie would pick up on its resonance. While I searched for the form, she went to the west window, watching a twin-engine plane land. When it had taxied away, she stared out at the sea, watching the grasses combed down by the wind. She moved to the other window, the mountain horizon of the Lake District capped with cloud.

When I'd found what I needed, we locked the clubhouse and tried to catch up with the others, who were already at the holding point. Shenton's plane was ready on the centre line, and without any delay the others hooked up the glider. By the time we reached them, I only had to check the straps. They were airborne moments later.

The turnaround that day was so rapid we didn't get much chance to talk. After the first run I showed Katie how to hook up the cable and got her to run the wing, then collect the cable a couple of times. We could pass only general comments about each flight and how the weather was holding out. It was after three when I told her she'd be next. She turned away and looked up at the glider as it broke away from the tow-plane.

Shenton flew over the end of the runway, detached the cable, then dropped for a short-landing. I listed the things she should remember, advising her to relax and enjoy it rather than try to be perfect. While we talked, it looked like Patrick was practising wing-overs, rather than giving a lesson, and when he was alarmingly low he pulled into the circuit, dipped a wing to keep it steady while landing in the crosswind, then rolled to a halt.

There's such a premium on staying airborne that newcomers are often shocked by the speed with which they're put inside, closed in and sent down the strip. In the two minutes it took to strap Katie in and send her off, I found myself becoming nervous, not out of fear but because I hoped she would enjoy it. She'd never flown before, not even in a 747, although I assured her that flying in a glider was nothing like being in a passenger plane anyway. Over the years we'd come across a few well-travelled types, the sort who read newspapers on takeoff to appear nonchalant. They were the ones most likely to be frightened by the exposed cockpit of a glider, feeling the suck and swell of sixty-degree banked turns. There was a chance the experience could affect Katie in that way, but as I saw the two aircraft take off as one, keeling up to the right, I chose not to worry.

I looked across the water to the Lucas garage, so small it was like any other coastal building, and felt certain that Katie was looking at it from the air. First-time fliers are often more impressed by seeing the familiar from a new angle than by the sensation of flight.

From the ground it's almost impossible to see a glider hitting a thermal, but you know when they've found one because the pilot circles in the rising air. A cool day in Barrow provides only lacklustre updraughts, so that the best Patrick could manage was to delay the descent. Twenty minutes later they were low enough to move on to the circuit and then came in to land. Patrick caught each lull and push of the crosswind and landed perfectly; the wing dropped only when the glider was at rest, with no scrape.

Katie thanked Patrick quietly, unbuckled her harness and stepped out to make room for the next flier. She backed away from the rush of activity, and I leaned in to Patrick.

'She's a natural,' he said. 'No skidding, no overcorrection. She'll solo in no time.'

I left the other students to sort themselves out and went over to Katie, who was standing alone. Briefly, it reminded me of the time Nicola had taken her first flight with us, years ago. Katie gave me the sort of smile that people manage when they feel like crying.

'I can't tell you . . .' she said, following it with a frustrated sigh. I wanted to say that I understood, that I was pleased she felt that way, but the tow-plane revved up, making it pointless to speak.

September was close, leaving only a few weeks of flying, but Katie said she'd join us until the season was over. The weather broke more often than it held, but she managed to push her hours up gradually. Patrick seemed more obsessed with her aviation abilities than with any potential she might have to join us in the rage. It was left to John and myself to seek out signs of continued renewal, but we never got much chance to be with her alone, and the weeks passed without much insight.

The strongest indication came on a night we all spent in the Lamb, and even Patrick was forced to notice her awareness. We hadn't been to the Lamb much during the summer, but Katie's return gave us more reason to go out as a group in the evenings. We'd gone from hardly seeing each other to having John, Patrick, Nicola, Katie and myself sitting around at night, talking about flying. John joined in as much as he could.

It was getting late when Katie became distracted by the space by the bay windows. It was months since I'd gathered the extended distortion from there, and I could sense nothing of it, but she appeared to be disturbed by something in that direction. She narrowed her eyes a few times, trying to focus, looking across as she drank.

Nicola was oblivious to this, but Patrick, John and myself found it difficult to talk about anything, because Katie was being so blatant. We weren't the only ones to have noticed; Ian was stationary behind the bar, fingering his beard with worry. He hadn't seen much of us, and now an obvious event was taking place while he watched.

During all this, Nicola talked directly to Katie, asking how her flying was going, and how long until she'd solo. Katie managed to reply, still glancing off to the side. They kept chatting, uneasily, both waiting for the rest of us to join in.

'Have I missed something?' Nicola asked.

'Nothing,' Patrick said, but then another silence followed.

'Does anybody want more to drink?' I asked, trying to get things moving.

'I can't face walking again,' Nicola said, because a few times recently we'd drunk so much that none of us had been able to drive. They hadn't been big nights, so it hadn't really been worth the effort of trudging home for the sake of one more beer.

Nicola said to Patrick, 'Perhaps we should go.' It was hushed, but not secret, and yet it had been directed only at him.

'I'd rather walk,' he said. 'And I need another drink.' A second later he offered me his keys.

'Does anybody want a lift?' I asked, feeling as though I'd been dismissed. Nicola accepted, but Katie shook her head.

John weighed up the beer in his glass, probably wondering if he should go for the free lift or try to get another pint. He opted for the lift.

When the cold hit me, outside, I was reminded of how similar it was to New Year. Once again, Nicola and I had left Patrick with Katie.

Nicola didn't speak until I'd dropped John off. The only thing she said before she got out was, 'I just worry for him, that's all.'

In the following weeks, Nicola came to me for friendship. Patrick still saw her for hours at a time, but now he talked openly to her about wanting to be with Katie. It was as though his time with Nicola had been an interlude, and she kept asking me for explanations. I never refused her company, because I enjoyed being near her, but her complaints were annoying.

We walked up to the Roundhouse in early October, the first time we'd been out for dinner together. It was only because neither of us could be bothered cooking. It wouldn't be dark for hours, but the light had clarified and shifted towards golden. I'd always thought that autumn light was created by sunset and leaves, but there were neither on that walk, and yet the air was thick with colour. Being low, the sun made everything full of long shadows as well as light; houses, grass, stones, even the waves, were lit on one side and dark on the other. I was standing on the light side of Nicola, her skin tanned from spending so much time at the airfield, her eyes wide.

'All this time I thought we were friends, but as soon as he gets the chance of fucking somebody, he's off.' She rarely swore at all, so she faltered over the words. 'It makes you wonder if that's all he wanted from me.'

'You were always the one that encouraged him to be with Katie.'

'He isn't actually with her, is he?'

'Not that I've heard.'

In truth, he'd already been rejected. That night when we'd left them at the Lamb, he'd told Katie how he felt, only realising the emotions as he said the words. She'd turned him down, and for some reason Patrick was able to laugh about that with me. I think I'd have started to feel sorry for myself in his position, but he said he was so glad she was around that it didn't matter what she said. He knew how they'd both felt that time at New Year, and he believed it would happen again. He wasn't going to be terminally patient, as he had been with Nicola, but persistent. 'You can't bask in somebody's attention without sharing what they feel,' he'd said confidently. I'd suggested that if it didn't work out by Christmas I'd sleep with him, and although he was sober he loved the idea. 'I will, you know,' he'd said. 'I'll have your arse. You think I'm joking, but it might come to that.'

I knew it was best not to tell Nicola that Patrick had confessed things to me, which he no longer told her. She didn't respond to what I'd said, but carried on talking.

'I wanted to be close to him, but did that mean I *had* to use my body? Isn't it possible to get near to somebody without having them inside you? It's the obligation to do it that bothers me. Couldn't we build something without having to go to bed straight away? It's always assumed that you will.'

'I don't think it was like that,' I said. 'He wasn't after sex, as such, but knew that if he did have sex with you it would mean something. Something about the future.'

'Sex as a way of claiming me?'

'Maybe it was just for the pleasure. Why miss the opportunity of enjoying yourselves more? Don't you ever just feel like having a shag?'

'All the time,' she laughed, 'but not with him. I think I'd rather have done it with a stranger than with somebody I cared about. I don't think a naked hour in bed could have accounted for how I felt.'

'You talk about emotions, though. You can't put all that down to friendship.'

'Did anybody ever consider that maybe he just didn't turn me on?'

If that had been said clinically, it would have been crude, but she sounded so sad, almost as though she wished she'd desired him.

'Patrick just wouldn't understand that. To him, there's nothing more erotic than feeling close to somebody.'

I hated that conversation, because I kept thinking that all I wanted to do was sleep with her. If she'd asked me why, I wouldn't have been able to give an explanation.

When we reached the Roundhouse the skinny man I'd seen before was by his car, but there was no sign of his dog. He'd run out of cigarettes, but his pacing continued.

Inside, I was surprised to find Suzette setting the tables.

Patrick had told me she'd left there weeks before. He'd met her in town, they'd gone for a drink and she'd talked about some other job. She must have been lying to him.

I hadn't talked to Suzette since that morning in bed. Once I'd woken, she'd said, 'We could have been anybody.' When I'd looked confused, she'd said, 'You'd rather have been with somebody else, and I'd rather have been with Patrick.' She'd apologised then, for sounding hurtful, but I'd told her not to worry. At the time I'd said that as long as we could be friends, it didn't matter, but neither of us had made any effort to see the other since.

We were polite to each other in the restaurant, but nothing like as friendly as the time I'd met her in the car park. She must have thought Nicola was my girlfriend. If she'd listened to our conversation, which went round in the same circles, she'd have known otherwise.

We stayed longer than planned, drinking another bottle of wine long after our food had gone. The restaurant emptied rapidly before we were ready to leave, but Suzette came over to suggest we order coffees if we wanted to stay longer. Nicola agreed, and even when those drinks had gone we stayed on while Suzette wiped down the tables. It was only towards the end of the night that we stopped talking about Patrick. I'd expected the conversation to turn more general, but for a good ten minutes she asked about me. I tried to give her an idea of how I worked, without actually giving away details of the rage. I knew I might end up sounding like Patrick to her, but that might not be a bad thing.

'That's a contradiction about you,' Nicola said, after I'd been talking for a while, and it felt peculiar for her to be weighing me up. 'You say you care about intuition, and the way things relate, and yet you don't appear to *feel* anything. Other than a sort of basic appreciation of the way things look.'

'I can't believe you think that.'

I thought for a moment that I'd have told her how I'd felt about her, if Suzette hadn't been there. But there was something else that held me back. For the first time, I understood how Patrick had managed to be patient. If I told her that I'd wanted to be with her for years, on and off, that would probably be the end of our friendship now.

It also occurred to me, briefly, that if I kept my feelings quiet, she might be more willing to risk a relationship with me. She had said she'd rather sleep with somebody who didn't move her.

She was talking, adding to what she'd said, but I couldn't hear her. When she stopped talking I said we should probably go.

'Aren't you going to say goodbye to your friend?' she asked, nodding towards the kitchen.

'Yes, all right.'

The kitchen was brightly lit, but it smelled of laundry more than food. I couldn't see the chef, but Suzette was sitting between two silvered tables on a wooden chair. One arm was across her stomach, the other holding her head up, eyes closed. She looked asleep, or perhaps upset, so I started to back away, but Nicola had walked up beside me. She gave a look of concern, and I nodded towards the door, suggesting we leave. I backed away, but when I'd made the space Nicola walked past me and knelt by Suzette. She put an arm around her back, whispering. I heard Suzette say that she was all right, but couldn't follow much more than that. I watched, expecting Suzette's pain to release, but whether she knew it or not Nicola was easing the emotion before it had chance to congeal. I went back to the main room and sat at our table.

When Nicola came back I asked her what was wrong.

'She's all right now. Come on.'

Autumn was clear, but the air was so cool that our glider fell straight through it. As usual, we kept flying longer than was practical, those flights lasting less than ten minutes because there was no lift. We wasted the tiny club profits on an excess of aero-tows. At least Shenton got to build his hours.

I did most of the flying, but Patrick stayed nearby, taking over whenever it was Katie's turn to go up. The reason he grounded himself the rest of the time was to be near her, so he'd take up about three flights, then hand back to me. I didn't think she'd even noticed this until an afternoon when Katie said, 'It can give you a headache, being stared at.'

'You think he stares?'

'It's not just staring. It's what he feels.'

I wanted to ask her if she could sense what he felt, to question the extent of her renewal, but it was something Patrick had warned me away from. If she was ever going to join the fold, he now claimed, it should be through him. He would get to know her better than anybody, and that trust would allow him to lead her into the rage. I kept arguing for a neutral induction and suggested that I be the initiator, but he kept repeating that he had to be the one. And it would happen soon. 'You've no idea how close she is,' he'd said. I never knew whether he'd sensed something in her, or was saying that to put me off.

He was uneasy about the end of the flying season,

knowing that his time with Katie might be reduced. There was one sunny day in early October when we took the glider out for its last day. Even if the weather stayed fine for another weekend, we felt the need to give up on the season officially. It was easier than hoping from weekend to weekend. Most of the students had given up by then anyway. On that last day, the air felt cold, but my skin was warmed with sunshine. The sun was so low that the sea was nothing but white glare. The flights were brief, but still and easy to control, so I spent most of the day up there while Patrick stayed with Katie.

Around mid-afternoon they walked away together. It was only five minutes to the water's edge, and the air there was warm, made tangy by the sea. Sitting a foot or so behind her, pretending to watch the water, Patrick absorbed all her movements. She breathed in, her chest rising. He felt as though she was on the verge of saying something, but she never spoke.

Water curled over itself, and the seagulls sang wildly then swooped down to land on the water.

Katie wrapped her arms around her thighs, linking her fingers, holding hands with herself. She leaned her body on to her legs, resting her head on her knees, eyes closed. Her lips were pressed against her knees. Almost kissing.

Nothing he could say would be any use, but he wanted to tell her that he'd given up, that she'd strained any sense of defence out of him, and that all he wanted to do was warm her.

Katie opened her eyes, and they were looking at him. Holding her gaze, he realised how rare it was for them to look at each other without one of them turning away.

She sat up and stared at her feet, dazed, as though she'd left a dream.

'Were you asleep?' he asked.

'I'm not sure,' she said. 'I thought I was somewhere else.'

They flew together an hour later, and there was less haze than there had been all summer. When the air is that clear, you're more aware of the space than when it's detailed with particles of mist; the clarity makes it feel like a deep mile of glass.

When she released the cable, climbing steeper than felt comfortable, there was enough quiet for Patrick to hear Katie's breathing. They banked over to the ocean horizon, flying directly towards a full moon, its seas as blue as the sky it rested in. Patrick could never let go of a belief that the moon only comes out at night. When he saw the full sphere of it in daytime, it felt like a reward.

He urged Katie to raise the nose.

'We've paid for this height, don't burn it all off.'

He guessed that she'd pushed the nose down because she was anxious to avoid stalling. If you fly slowly with the nose raised, the wing no longer splits the air around itself but hits it like a wall. The lift breaks away, and at that moment a wing is said to stall – the nose drops to the ground and you dive. If the wings aren't kept level, the aircraft can twist into spin. Close to the ground, a stall will kill you, so it's essential that a trainee pilot learns stall-recoveries. You should never stall by accident, so a recovery should never be necessary, but by practising stalls you learn to recognise the signs of their onset: a deeper quiet, sloppy controls and a thudding in the wings. Patrick's repeated attempts to cure her tension had served only to make her more nervous, but he couldn't solo her until she was confident stalling.

That afternoon he told Katie to stay on the same

heading, then asked her to stall the glider. Reluctantly, she brought the nose up, the moon vanishing beneath the instrument panel, the wings shuddering. It was a wishy-washy attempt, and they sat there in the pre-stall buffet, refusing to drop. In some ways she was right to pull up gently, because a fast pullback will bring on a fierce stall. She was trying to keep it bearable. Patrick pulled back a bit more, and there was a sigh from the wings as they gave up flying. It felt as though they'd been dropped, and the horizon arced up again, the moon a blur, a rush of ground filling the view.

'Recover,' Patrick said, and Katie pushed the stick forward to regain control, then coaxed the glider level.

'Good. But as soon as you get airspeed, pull up.'

They flew towards the moon again, and perhaps because they'd lost some height it looked larger, the sky around it darker. There was a brief stillness, but then they hit some rough air. They dropped slightly, and then the glider was nose down, pointing straight at the clear ocean.

'I've got it,' Patrick yelled, but Katie had already let go. The stick was fully forward. Mistaking the rough air for a stall, she'd pushed the stick forward, and they'd slammed into a dive.

The pressure of the dive turned Patrick's vision grey, and the wings were screaming. He felt heavy, as if he was lying on his back in the sun, and his face was warm. His head felt thick with blood, hands too weak to hold the stick. He heard Katie moan, her lungs letting go of air with the force of the drop. At that speed, you can't pull up rapidly because you'll either get an accelerated stall or airframe failure. You have to coax it out of the dive, no matter how rapidly an impact is approaching.

Patrick had heard pilots say that in an emergency you

don't swear or panic, but concentrate on survival. He proved that to be untrue, swearing at Katie through gritted teeth as he carefully dragged them out of the dive, levelling off at nine hundred feet.

'What were you doing? Fuck.'

She didn't answer, and in moments they were lined up with the runway, the frost having melted from it in patches.

From ground level the moon looked lower, pale in the white space above the horizon. They rolled to a halt, and the wing settled to the ground.

'What the fuck were you doing?'

'I thought it was a stall. I tried to correct it.'

'Fuck, Katie, it was negative G. You have to get used to that. You can't fly if you're that scared of stalling. You could have torn the wings off.'

He was more disappointed with himself for reacting badly than he was with her.

None of us felt like celebrating, but we had a tradition of taking the students out for a drink at the end of the season. By nine o'clock Patrick was pissed and kept disappearing. I'd find him talking to people he'd never met before, or intruding on conversations. When he came back to our table, he'd be quiet.

Nicola had joined us, but she looked pale, as though she was getting flu. I kept asking how she was, almost hoping she'd get ill so I could look after her. She kept telling me there was nothing wrong, but that she probably ought to go home soon. Nobody left for another hour. When Patrick said he couldn't take much more, it was a signal for everybody to leave.

It was frosty outside, and the cold air must have been

too much for Patrick, because by the time we'd followed him out he was motionless, trying not to be sick. Katie offered to walk him home, but we made her call a taxi.

'Don't worry,' I told her. 'He does this every year. The only miracle is that I'm not doing the same thing.' It wasn't exactly true, but we usually ended up in some sort of a state once the flying was over.

It was too cold to be standing around, and the students left as a group, looking friendlier than they had done all year. Nicola said she'd wait with me, and we stood there silently, blowing into our hands, while Katie made an attempt to keep Patrick occupied. She'd moved him a couple of yards away, so he was out of the pub's light. You could see their breath, catching in the glare as it came away from them. Through that haze, Patrick appeared to be standing straight now, talking clearly, probably feeling better for having found some space. I couldn't make out much, except the shine of his hair. Katie was reaching up, putting her fingers through it, placing one palm on his face. The breath around them stopped, because they were kissing. It was brief, and after that he pulled Katie against his chest as though she was the one who was ill.

I couldn't bring myself to look at Nicola, but she said, 'I don't think he remembers.'

The taxi arrived, and they got in without speaking to us.

'He was with me,' Nicola said. 'Earlier tonight. Outside the toilets. We were only there for a few minutes, but it happened.'

The full moon was melted out of shape by street-lit clouds. At ground level the air was still, but the sky was racing. I'd been unable to sleep well, repeating dreams and trying to remember something that bothered me. It had felt like a whole night of disturbance, but when I'd finally woken the clock said 4a.m. Once I'd seen that, I knew that sleep would evade me until dawn, so I made the most of it by going out.

It was only as I walked that the reason for my disturbed sleep occurred to me. It wasn't Nicola's time with Patrick that bothered me, but her response to Suzette a few days earlier. She'd done more good than we ever could have done by collecting the pain. It made me worry that we might merely be patching up the town rather than contributing to its health. I didn't let it concern me for long, because I knew that without our cleansing Barrow would be in a worse state. Even so, it wasn't something I'd want to discuss with the others.

At that time of morning, the houses down my road were still. You can tell when people are asleep, not just by the darkness but by a settling that occurs in the air around their homes. One house was lit by a television, its curtains open, but other than that there were no signs of life.

Crossing on to the mainland, I let the route unravel before me. Focusing on my surroundings wasn't easy, because introspection is a night-time reflex. When the activity of the day lessens, it's natural to turn inwards, especially if it's dark. You can walk for miles, daydreaming, seeing nothing of your route. It took an effort to stop myself from thinking about Katie and Nicola and to pay attention to the town.

From the promenade I walked towards the metalwork chimneys on the south shore. Their segments were bound together by what looked like thread, though I knew the cable was as wide as my arm. It was cold passing the docks, the flat-decked ships so high they obscured most of the sky. Despite the ships' size, there's something ragged about their appearance when they are being built, with too many bundles of tubing and rope arranged in their frames. I followed the path along the docks, never tempted by the wide road bridges that led into the mass of channels around the harbours. At that proximity, even the Vickers building was dwarfed by the ships. Above me, the wide booms of cranes looked like inverted boat skeletons, their hollow struts making the wind rumble. Further down, warehouses had been converted into luxury flats, but they'd never sold, so their windows were swirled over with white paint.

Moving back into town, I felt anxious because I'd seen no traces of pain on my walk. It's usually the best time to find it, alone in the dark, but there was nothing. I tried to imagine that one of the others had been out before me, but it was unlikely.

I found a backstreet that led towards the Arcadia Bookshop, past the Larches Estate. The shops there didn't appear to know what sort of products they wanted to sell, each displaying an assortment of porcelain dogs, brass coal scuttles, clothes pegs and laundry baskets. The exception was a ballet shop, with shelves of point shoes looking pleasantly hard beneath the droop of ribbon laces. Next door there was an empty shop, its entrance boarded up. The window was plastered with cardboard, but I looked through a gap; in the centre of the room there was a red lampshade. It was plugged into a wall socket, but remained unlit.

Heading west again, I stopped at the sports centre, because the lights had been left on in the gym, illuminating the Peace Garden. The council's idea of tranquillity was only the size of a back yard, with one bench, a rockery and a huge, coarsely hewn sculpture of praying hands. Set between the main road and the gym, the garden was usually dark enough to attract drunks. The floor was rough with broken bottles, caked with trodden dog shit and vomit. The air was dewy, and something nearby smelled like roses and milk. It was so slight a smell that if I inhaled too deeply the speed of my breathing made it undetectable. I assumed it must have been a plant, but couldn't locate the source.

Headlights lit the road, and I stepped back into the darker part of the garden. From behind the bench I saw the beam of the headlights fragment. There was a slur in the light close to the bench, and I could make out faint traces of a swollen distortion. It was much larger than a thread of pain and reminded me of the one I'd retrieved in the Lamb in March. Its skin was so fine I could have missed it quite easily, but I could tell it was an abnormal trace. It didn't spread horizontally, but sagged and spiked into the air. When the car had gone, I sat on the bench and leaned forward into the edge of the stain.

Expecting it to be empty, as the last one had been, I was surprised to feel a pressure of pain stored within it. My mind clouded with overlapping images and feelings; a telephone box surrounded by the glittered remnants of its shattered windows; water being blown under a front door, staining a carpet black; the body of a cat matted into roadside grass. It was as though this hollow distortion had soaked up the feelings of those who came to the garden in pain; there were accusations, words of blame, faces twisted in anger, doors slammed and hours alone.

Too many events to read completely. The last of the bulge settled inside me.

I should have been worried about who could craft such a distortion, or why they would do so. More than anything, though, I was bothered by the way it had made me feel. I hadn't taken pleasure in the pain, exactly, but I'd been thrilled by its intensity. I remembered what Nicola had said about me never feeling anything. At the time, I'd thought she was ridiculous, but she may have had a point. I'd been so focused on Patrick's displays of suffering that I'd never allowed my own feelings to rise. I should have been furious with loss, but impatience had numbed me.

I allowed the distortion I'd taken in to rise, eager for its sensation. We'd always been told it was impossible to be your own victim, to conduct the rage alone, but I found myself kneeling, hands becoming fists. My teeth bit hard enough for me to taste blood, arms cramping against my chest, but even as the pain was released, there was no sound, not even of breathing.

4   Phlogiston

With Patrick remaining free of pain for the next rage, I spent a few days walking around with John, collecting pain. Occasionally, we went further afield in his car, but that was partly because November was freezing, and we didn't want to spend as much time walking. At the end of the week I asked him to drive me to an out-of-town house. I could have borrowed his car, but I wanted him to be there because there could be such a mess when we arrived. John drove with one hand, using the other to rub his nails over his lips, then to push his glasses back up. It was a movement I'd seen him make even when his glasses were off, so it was probably nothing more than habit.

The southern road to Ulverston ebbed back and forth from the coastline, sometimes at sea level or cresting the shallow hills. The only striking sights were the bundled metal of the gasworks and the white block of Heysham's nuclear reactor on the coast. There was a handful of houses, built behind banks of soil and stone. Most had hand-written signs attached to their gates, offering potatoes, mussels and oysters. I looked out to sea, where there were three silhouettes of men rocking their tread-planks on the waterlogged sand-flats, tossing their catch into shoulder baskets.

John turned left into a tree-lined lane, the ground around the bare trees rotten with leaf matter. I was guessing directions, feeling my way to the building rather than remembering.

'Have you been here before?' he asked.

'Not to this house, but nearby. There should be a right turn in those trees.'

'It feels like we're miles from town,' he complained. 'Isn't this too far away for us to be bothering with?'

'No, it's fine. There's the turn.'

It was difficult trying to talk about anything other than our direction, and I could sense that John was nervous. I didn't know whether it was my plan that bothered him or being alone with me. He turned up the next right, leaning forward, looking up through the trees to the pylons beyond.

'We won't even be trespassing,' I assured him, knowing how he hated going anywhere he wasn't allowed. He was terrified of being caught in abandoned places, to the extent of avoiding car parks and warehouses at night. We'd never managed to get him to come on a factory run, which was probably a good thing. When you're on a secret retrieval, you don't want to be with somebody who is liable to panic.

We were looking for an abandoned farmhouse. The family had reputedly moved back to Scotland after the farmer had shot himself, and the land was up for sale. It wasn't the suicide I was interested in so much as the chance to gain access to a private building. There were some houses in and around Barrow that had been occupied for decades without any of us being able to gain entry.

When a private dwelling was opened up we couldn't miss the opportunity to clear it out. There was always the chance that such untouched spaces would be so far gone we'd be unable to heal them, but if they had only been mildly tarnished it felt like our duty to clear them out. In town, that was easier, because one of our group could always find an excuse to examine a building, but it felt a bit more risky when you were on farmland.

The gate was open, but John stopped the car before we reached it, as though it represented a threshold he was reluctant to cross. The house was made of slate-coloured bricks, mostly hidden in ivy. Its back wall was being used to support an overflow of junk from the nearby barn: tyres, plywood crates, a rust-damaged plough. No signs said it was for sale, but I went to the back door and found it unlocked. There was no way we'd find any physical evidence of the suicide, I assured myself, not even a stain, so I went inside. Behind me, John glanced from side to side, then stopped to listen. When he was sure there was nobody around he followed me.

'Do you want to share this one?' he asked, knowing I could claim the house for myself.

'That's why you're here.'

The place smelled of bleach and something like damp biscuit crumbs, which I presumed came from the old carpets. The furniture had been removed, which made the building feel colder than it was outside. John went upstairs, so I checked the rooms around me; a clammy kitchen, two wide bare rooms, a spare toilet. That last room was unusually cold, though I could find no source for the apparent draught.

The thought of taking on so much pain was unpleasant, and I wondered if this reluctance was affecting my concentration, because I was unable to bring anything into view. It's rarely easy to see the threads in daylight, but given time and patience they can be urged to appear, especially in shadows.

John's footsteps moved to another location above me. I tried scanning the rooms from different angles but still couldn't see any traces. In the calmest of houses there is usually something to be gained, but the air was spotless.

There was a bang from upstairs, a door slammed. After a pause, John came down the stairs, his feet scuffing on the bare wood.

'Nothing up there either?' I asked.

'No.' He breathed into his hands. It looked like a nervous gesture, more than a need for warmth. 'What's going on?'

'Somebody's beaten us to it.'

A storm had been building since mid-afternoon, and by sundown the clouds looked like they'd been dipped in mud. It didn't take long for the darkness to thicken, with the onset of lightning a few minutes before the rain. I wanted to see Patrick but was put off by the sound of the weather. I made my mind up to visit him when the power cut out, all the lights down my street dimming at once. The murmur of the fridge slowed to nothing, leaving the sound of wind-blown rain against the front of the house. I wasn't cold but didn't want to spend the whole night in darkness, listening to thunder, so put my coat on and headed to the mainland. Before I made it to the end of my road, some rooms were being lit by candles, wobbly shadows moving as the flames were set in place.

I hadn't owned an umbrella for years, because they don't last more than five minutes in coastal winds, but wished I had some protection from the rain. My coat offered a few minutes of body-warmth, but my trousers and jumper were soon as wet as my hair.

The mainland streetlights were on, indicating that, as usual, the power cut had affected only the island. The worst of the storm was a few miles inland, lightning striking several times a minute. There's a contradiction about lightning; some of the brightest forks are followed by nothing other than a slow sound like falling rubble. Other times, the smallest flashes can rend the sky with a tearing sound. That night the sounds were mostly long and low, except when I was on the Jubilee Bridge, feeling more exposed than I would have liked. It was the bluest strike, a vertical column fixing in the air behind the town, softening for a second as afterimage. I could tell that the sound was about to follow and braced myself as the volume burst around me. The vibration settled in my lungs as a hum.

When I reached Patrick's it was a relief to see light from his living room, and I knocked on the window, then the door. The curtains parted, closed again, and I moved closer to the door, trying to use the house to avoid the rain. It was easing slightly, more noise coming from overflowing drains and the rush of streams in gutters than from droplets hitting the ground. Patrick's outside light came on, its domed bulb sheathed with wet cobwebs. When he opened the door, the dazzle of rain around me made it difficult to see into the unlit hall, but he looked pleased to see me.

'You're a mad sod,' he said. 'Get a car.'

My hair was wet enough to run water over my face, but my clothes were soaked in moisture rather than dripping. I followed him into his kitchen. The fluorescent strip light flickered, making metallic sounds; the light looked like a white flame spreading down the tube, never quite taking. He had to switch it off and on again to make it ping on fully.

'Do you fancy going out for a drink when I've dried off?'

'Maybe,' he said, looking at my wet clothes. He smiled, almost laughing as he watched me wiping the water from my face. I smiled back, because it was a long time since I'd seen him look happy.

'There's something we should talk about,' I said.

'Go on.'

I told him the story of the suicide house, giving him all the details in case he was able to focus on something I'd missed.

'And John saw this as well?' he asked.

'Yes.'

I wanted to tell him about the distortion I'd found at the Peace Garden, but given the way I'd let the rage take me it would have felt too much like a confession. I felt sure it had been spawned deliberately, put into that location to draw half-formed pain out of people, gathering whatever misery was strewn in the surroundings. Whoever had put it there must have intended to burn off that pain in self-rage, as I had done. I didn't feel any less guilty for knowing that, because I'd allowed the rage to come when I should have stored the events. I now suspected that whoever was setting up these distortions was also raiding pain from the town. What they intended to do with the residue, I didn't want to guess. Sooner or later, though, the other members of our group would notice, and the subject would be talked about.

'I'm having difficulty getting my head around all this,'

Patrick said. 'We should get out. Do something else. I don't want to stay in all night. And I don't want to get drunk.'

'You're not seeing Katie?'

'Not tonight.'

I didn't know whether to believe him. We'd been out three times since he'd been seeing Katie, and every time he'd ended up walking over to her flat and spending the night there. 'It seems pointless,' he'd admitted, 'because I go straight to sleep and then she leaves before I wake up. But she never complains about me being there.' From the way he talked about it, their relationship seemed unreasonably dull. He elaborated on this as we drove.

Without a particular direction in mind, he'd set off, saying we should find somewhere good to walk. Driving inland we saw that the storm had blown itself out, and the horizon had lightened. Sunlight came under the clouds and caught in their bases like flame-coloured mist. At ground level, the wet made everything shine, the fields flaring beneath the dark cloud.

'What happens when you get what you want?' Patrick asked.

'Happiness? Disappointment? Ennui?' I was trying to make him laugh, but he'd have none of it.

'Anger,' he said. 'I feel angry with her for having made me want her so much.'

'Katie didn't make you do anything. And you spent most of this year trying to be with somebody else.'

He breathed out as though blowing smoke, shaking his head. He knew his argument made no sense but couldn't think of an alternative. His voice was stiff as he said, 'But I feel angry.'

'Perhaps you're angry because you expected something else. After all that build-up, it should have felt like more.'

'I still have those feelings,' he said, 'but it's as though being with her makes no difference. I'm still longing for something that hasn't been resolved.'

'To bring her on?'

'No,' he said firmly, as though it no longer interested him.

It looked too wet to walk, and the sun had gone down, but Patrick pulled over, parking next to a field with no footpaths. It felt still, but I could hear wind in the grass and trees. In that sort of weather, twilight couldn't last long, and we'd soon be cold, but he said, 'We don't do this often enough,' so I followed him.

I'd expected to walk through the open fields, but everywhere he went was a borderline place, along hedges, fences, derelict walls that might once have been barns. We walked by the edge of woods that were dark, apart from the fluorescent light of a distant farm that came through in fragments. We didn't talk, because it felt like he was leading me somewhere. I was getting cold and impatient.

'What is it you're looking for?'

'You know, we're a million miles from all this most of the time. We get so wrapped up in what's happening, we forget all this potent stuff that's going on.'

It didn't feel like we'd seen anything of great significance, but I could sense that Patrick was looking, and that the night meant more to him. We ended up in a space between two fields, where a wooden bridge had been built over a ditch. There was a distinct whiff of charcoal, as though an old fire had been rained on. It made me unaccountably nervous.

'What's the point of all this?' I asked.
'We can make things happen.'
'Meaning?'
'Haven't you ever thought of using the rage, for more than just looking at things? I think some of the others probably do. John's often said things about looking after his health.'
'I don't think he meant that.'
'Then what?'
I didn't have an answer.
It was possible that Patrick had planned to show me something more, but changed his mind when he saw my reaction. Or it could have been that there was nothing to see, and he was also getting tired. I found it difficult to read him, but I was surprised when he said we should go back. I hadn't sensed anything unusual out there, except Patrick himself, but made a note of the locations in case I ever needed to come back. Walking to the car, he changed the subject and carried on where we'd left off earlier. It didn't sound like a conversation that was occurring to him as he spoke so much as something he'd been planning on telling me.
'When you get what you want,' he said, out of breath, 'you ruin it. Not because you're afraid of losing it, but because you can. Because it's more interesting to create a drama, to make your life feel important.'
'What have you done to ruin it?'
He told me that a few hours earlier, Nicola had gone round to his house. He'd not seen her alone for weeks, but within half an hour they were in bed. I'd been worried by his mood, but this helped to explain it. The realisation took a moment to hit me.
He stopped, looking at the sky, watching the stars; his

gaze kept moving from side to side, so it looked as though he was reading out loud to me.

'I don't think she really wanted to. It was strange, because nothing happened at first. We didn't fall into each other's arms, but talked about it. She was sitting in the front room with me, and she said she wanted to have sex. We *agreed* to it. And then we had to start, cold. She even said, "Come on then", and I had to start touching her. Can you imagine that? I thought it was going to be a disaster, but then . . .'

'You enjoyed it more than with Katie?'

He started walking again.

'I felt even less. I couldn't lose myself in the moment. It was just so weird seeing a familiar face on a naked body. She left about ten minutes before you came round. When you knocked on the door I thought she'd come back. Did you know?'

'I had no idea.'

'You're taking it pretty well,' he said, giving me the first indication that he'd known about my own desire.

'And yourself?'

'Cracking up,' he said. 'Whatever else, I've ruined it with Katie now. I had those feelings, and I pissed on them.'

We didn't talk after that, and I wondered if he could feel how tempted I was to spew rage at him. I wasn't particularly angry with him or Nicola — who could blame them? — but damage was occurring within me. If I hurt somebody else, I wouldn't feel as much for myself. It reminded me of a man I'd seen punching a lamppost on a Saturday evening. Even when his fingers had gone soft, he'd kept pounding his hand into the concrete. There'd been no fury about his movement, no grimace or strain;

you could tell that breaking himself in a small way was completely necessary.

I'd been collecting from funerals and hospitals that week and was so full of aftermath I could have brought it out in an instant. Patrick would have been brought to his knees in a second, but I resisted. Patrick was the next victim of the rage, so even if I did attack him with pain, it wouldn't matter much. It would be a shock, but he'd cope. Only if he'd been collecting pain would it have affected him. Even so, I let the stored pain come to my surface, hoping he might sense it.

In doing so, I picked up some of the memories from the funerals. There was no petty jealousy in that pain, no misery over girlfriends and boyfriends. It was pure, agonising loss. People had died, and they were going to be missed. The memories made my worries about Nicola seem insignificant, and helped to calm me down. When we got back in the car I didn't even slam the door.

Dreams are as unreliable as the weather. You can't trust them to tell you anything, but they can change the way you feel.

The night after Patrick's revelation, I dreamed about him being at the airfield. In the dream, he was taxiing a red aeroplane. Something was wrong with the wings, because fuel was pouring out of them. Patrick lined it up in the centre of the runway and pushed the throttle to maximum. Fuel fell and coated the tarmac behind him, making icy puddles that glared pink in the sunset light. The last of the fuel foamed from the wings until they only trailed drips. The plane's movement loosened as it rose from the runway. That was the moment Patrick always enthused about, when you break from the earth, and the weight of the aircraft slips into a drift. He climbed steeply, still heading towards us, but before he reached fifty feet the propeller caught; an instant later I heard the engine cut out as the last of the fuel was spent. There was probably enough room for him to drop the nose and make a short landing, but he turned, gliding around to his left. The angle of bank was so steep that he passed in front of me, side on, like a cross, losing height in the turn. As he levelled out, the left wing sliced into the blue glass of the control tower, turning it white. There was no noise as the glass fell away. The impact pulled the remains of the plane around on itself, folding it together before it hit the ground, where it rolled, lost in dust, and came apart as though made from sticks and rags. When the remains settled they looked like a wind-damaged tent. A wind blew the dust from the wreckage, and you could see Patrick standing in a clear space. As the sound returned there was only the smallest noise of wind moving the fragments of broken aeroplane over the grass. There was a powerful stink of fuel and smoke, but I could also smell the grass.

If I'd dreamed about him dying, I'd have taken it as a basic wish-fulfilment dream, a resentment playing itself out to a logical conclusion. But it reminded me of something else. It didn't seem wrong for him to have survived, but I felt that instead of standing still he should have been running. The momentum should have made him run, as the aeroplane came away from him.

It snowed for days, then froze and snowed again, until the whole town seemed to be at rest. Down my road, every house had at least one light on, because nobody went out. I didn't like being stuck in and would sit by the window, watching what little activity there was. A white cat made its way down the footpath, looking sulphurous against clean snow. It was treading carefully, looking nervous and confused, shaking the cold from its paws with each step. Across the road a brave, wrapped-up man came out and cleared the snow from his car, then shovelled a passage to the road. He poured a kettle full of water over the windscreen and attempted to start the engine. When the battery went dead he went inside, the last movement I saw for half an hour.

Bored senseless, I eventually walked into town, but by the time I was there I felt tired and cold. I had nowhere to aim for, nobody I wanted to see. It was good to see snow at the same time as Christmas trees, even though it wasn't quite December, but other than that it was a cheerless afternoon, so it was a relief to see a chestnut seller. He was huddled in shadow by the walls that ran down the side of the shopping centre, in an area so dark it was difficult to make him out. His movement was slow, cold-looking. When the wind caught the charcoal in his brazier, grey ash flaked off, and it shone like Christmas-tree lights. His face and hands didn't look dirty so much as thick-skinned, fingers pushing the chestnuts over the grate, turning them until they split. I asked for a bag full, and he shuffled them up and handed them over without looking at me.

Feeling pleased with my purchase, I managed to peel the wooden skin from the chestnuts while walking, the hard edges stabbing under my nails. They were so well cooked that the yellow flesh was creamy, almost like a mild cheese. I ate them before they had cooled, burning my fingertips. It was a simple pleasure, something that must have been experienced by a hundred other people that afternoon, but I felt grateful.

I'd walked away without direction and found myself in an empty street that ran behind the Larches Estate. Uncertain of where to go next, I stopped. There was a stillness, the light settling around me. I stood for a long time with no movement. Where there had been a breeze flickering litter in the gutters, there was calm. Nobody else was around, and I looked at the walls on either side, each window in the buildings. Instead of glancing around, my head was still, gaze fixed, but my perception widened so that I could see more. It was bright, everything appearing to be slightly haloed, but I didn't squint. I became aware of my body; the pain of chestnut pericarp under my fingernails; charcoal flavour in my mouth from the scorched kernels; a smell of burned coal, warm soot. I felt dryness on my cheeks, the skin tanned by cold. My heart slowed, thumping in response to the deeper opening of my lungs.

I blinked for the first time in minutes, and my eyes watered. As I walked on, wiping my face, I almost forgot what had happened. It was the same as waking from a strange dream. Once remembered, it is unforgettable, but almost, almost, you let it go in your rush to wake up.

From there I walked straight to Suzette's. I hadn't seen her since the night when Nicola had eased her discomfort at the Roundhouse, and that felt like a shame. Given the cold and the tiredness in my body, I could think of nothing better than spending an afternoon with her. The lad from the lower flat let me in and sent me up the stairs to Suzette's room. She opened her door enough to ask who it was, then she said, 'Thank God. I'm going mad in this place.'

As she let me in I was surprised to see she was wearing a white T-shirt and knickers, her hair down but messy, and I realised she'd been in bed. She said, 'Just wait while I get dressed', but then hunted through her clothes on the floor until she located a pack of Marlboros. She moved to the kitchen section of the room, holding the toaster's lever down, making the wires inside glow red. She lit a cigarette on them, then sucked at it and went back to sit on the bed cross-legged. Like most people, she'd been stuck inside for a few days, because the snow seemed like too much trouble, and she was bored. I imagined sitting there talking while she smoked all afternoon, but as soon as she finished, she said, 'We've got to get outside.' She was dressed minutes later, and we were outside. This time the cold felt refreshing rather than enervating, and there seemed to be more sunlight in the air.

We walked on the promenade by the docks, where the shadows on the aircraft carrier were lit with the sparks of welding. The steel chimneys in the south gave off a breathy smoke. I enjoyed the feel of cold on my lips, the tension in my bones. The light on the pavement was clear and sharp.

'We're casualties of each other,' Suzette said, looking at me briefly, then out to the island. 'We understand each other. Solidarity.'

I'd always feared she was dull, and now she was saying things that pleased me, even though I didn't know exactly what she meant.

'Casualties?'

'I spent months thinking about Patrick, even after I'd been with you. It took me a long time to realise I was missing you as well.'

'I'm glad about that.'

'We have nothing in common,' she said. 'I'll probably bore you to death before long.'

She'd assumed we'd be seeing more of each other, and I had no reason to be surprised or to disagree, because I must have assumed the same thing in going round to see her. Having slept with each other before, we didn't waste the day in build-up, but talked. We spent most of the afternoon in a café near the Jubilee Bridge.

Before it went dark she said that the restaurant needed her, but she asked me not to go home.

'I think we need each other tonight,' she said.

She drove us over to the Roundhouse, sat me at a corner table and brought food and drink to me all night. I should have been at the clubhouse, because it was the night of the rage. I could almost see it from where I was sitting, and it was strange to think of Patrick kneeling in agony while I enjoyed warmth and company. It meant I'd be carrying the stored pain longer than was wise, but I preferred to take the time off. Given the way he'd been recently, I was sure he'd have revelled in this particular rage, and I didn't want to be a part of it.

Suzette and I didn't get much chance to talk, but I enjoyed being near her. It was peculiar, being attracted to somebody who was so much the opposite of what I usually liked. Even when we went back to my house, she smoked as she undressed. Once she was naked she switched the lights off, opened the curtains to let in streetlight, and inhaled the last of her cigarette as she climbed on top of me. The ash sizzled as she stubbed it out in the empty packet and the smoke around her cleared.

When we'd slept together a month before, it had felt more like a mutual wank than a shared experience. This time, I could tell she was with me. Until then, I'd never detected any tenderness in her, but she held on to my face, kissing gently, then hard, then gently again. I couldn't take my eyes off her. She was coated in streetlight, and leaned back to breathe in, widening the slate-coloured shadows of her ribs. I expected her head to be thrown back, but saw the ends of her hair floating in front of her chest, and then her face became visible, eyes wide, looking into mine, her chin pressed against her collarbone. She must have turned from the light then, because her details were lost in shadow. Her eyes, throat and nipples were so dark they merged with the background. For a moment it was like looking through her.

On a relatively warm night for December, I walked around some of my favourite places. At the ballet shop, the flow of pink shoes and ribbons looked unchanged. Next door to this I paused by the closed-down shop. It had been standing empty for years now. The window was boarded up where the lower section had been kicked in. It wasn't a hole large enough for a person to fit through, so I assumed it had been smashed out of badness. The hole in the cardboard that I'd looked through last time had been Sellotaped up. It roused my curiosity to the extent that I wanted to get inside.

I crossed the road to the Peace Garden to get a better look at the building, making sure the rooms on either side and above were unoccupied. When I was satisfied that the surroundings were empty, I went back to try the door. It felt heavy, perhaps even nailed shut from the inside. The street wasn't busy – I counted three other people – but I needed privacy to find a way in, so I made my way to the back alley. There wasn't even any need to climb into the yard, because the back gate was unlocked.

The windows were grilled over, the wire-glass behind them shattered but still in place. The door looked solid, but after a quick check around I kicked it hard and it went in first time. It jammed against piles of newspapers, which helped to soften the noise.

It's strange how an unoccupied space smells bad. It's as though the presence of people cleanses a location; simply by breathing the air, we transport atmosphere and life into buildings, and make them feel lived in. The abandoned shop smelled more like a cold shed or barn, the carpet feeling like packed soil. I touched the walls, the painted plaster slick with damp.

My eyes were adjusting slowly, but I didn't want to spend more than a minute or so in there. I went through to the front section and saw outlines of streetlight around the hardboard coverings, implying that I'd made it through to the right place. I looked down to see the shape of the lampshade. I couldn't find a switch, so I felt along the flex to the wall socket and clicked it on. Looked at from above, the bulb glared white, so I crouched to appreciate the red glow. It was a risk to leave the light on, and I would have switched it off immediately, except that it illuminated a pattern on the far wall. Scraped into the wallpaper, perhaps with a nail, was a set of twelve sigils arranged in a circle. They were joined by lines, each to the other. The floor was dark, but I couldn't tell whether that was from damp or burning.

I heard sirens, at least two police cars coming closer, and switched the lamp off. I didn't know if I'd been discovered, but there was no point in staying any longer. As I stood to leave, the cable caught on my foot and the lamp fell over, the hot bulb smashing.

I hurried out the back, pausing only to make sure that

the alley was clear, then turned and followed the road towards the town centre. The sirens sounded further away now, but I could see blue flashes reflecting off windows.

On the footpath ahead of me I could make out a man crawling away from the main road. One arm was clutched around his waist, and I was struck by the absolute silence around him. He looked to be in agony, and there was a patchy black trail behind his legs. I expected gasps, but he didn't sound to be breathing. These thoughts passed in a fraction of a second, while another part of me rushed forward to help him. His shirt was blackened with blood, so wet it was shining. He must have been rubbing at his face, because the blood had spread all over it, making his eyes look wide. When I held his shoulders, telling him to relax, the sound returned and his breath wheezed out.

Pulling his shirt open was much harder than I'd imagined, the buttons refusing to tear off, and each tug made him wince. His teeth showed for a while, but then as I gained access to his belly he looked tired and still. His breathing had settled, sounding wet, like somebody who needs to cough. I couldn't tell whether he'd been stabbed or merely cut, but there were several wounds across his belly.

The sirens were further away. I wanted to shout for help but was having difficulty getting enough breath. A couple, holding hands, passed at the end of the street. I called at them to get the police, shouted that the man had been stabbed, but they walked away. They looked like a quiet type, so I hoped they would at least call for help, even if I'd scared them.

As I looked down the street, visualising an ambulance, willing one to appear, I saw a fibre of pain that the man had left behind him. It came from the end of the street, following a zigzagged path through the gutter and back on to the pavement. I looked down to his head, where the pain was still feeding out. I wanted to take it from him, but I was already so crammed with disorder that it would be unwise to take any more. Instead, I sat behind him and let him lean into my lap. His head felt like a wet boulder as I stroked it, but the movement helped to calm him.

'It's all right,' I said.

He murmured something, sounding as though I'd convinced him. Then his eyes closed, and he said, 'You should have *seen* her.'

I didn't have time to think about what he'd said, because an ambulance turned into the street, its headlights shining over us. As gently as I could I laid him down and walked away as the paramedics came forward. Once they were with him, I slipped back down the alley.

On Christmas Eve it had rained so hard the air was like fog. Nobody had ever seen rain like that, and people rang each other up to talk about it. When the weather's so unique, you almost expect something to happen. Patrick said later that he almost knew what was coming. He went to the Lamb with Katie and spent the night asking her if anything was wrong. She kept saying no, until last orders, when she told him it was over.

'There was all this tinsel and merriment, and she chose that moment. I respected her sense of drama,' he told me dryly on a night out in January

When he asked her why, Katie didn't have an answer. She kept saying things such as, 'There's no reason. I just don't want to any more.'

His story concerned me, because such a sudden change made me wonder what Katie was going through. I didn't want to leave it much longer before bringing her into the rage, and knew I couldn't leave it to Patrick any more.

'You get this greed of deep need,' he told me, 'and you forget what it was that you liked in the person. Half the time I'm so angry with her, even though I'm the one who fucked it up.'

'Patrick, she doesn't know that.'

'But it makes a difference. She doesn't know the reason, but it's because of what I did. She senses it.'

'You're reading too much into this.'

'What you do is more important than what you feel, or your intentions. It's no good saying "I love you" if you treat the person like shit.'

'You didn't treat her like shit.'

'This time last year,' he said, 'things were actually happening. Can you remember all that potential? Now it feels like everything's been spent.'

I wanted to tell him that I didn't care about what was happening with all these people. I cared that he was no longer taking TVs to bits, or coming up with ridiculous ideas. He hadn't even talked about flying since October.

We were sitting in the Lamb, getting drunker than was advisable. I'd wanted to tell him about the room I'd found, and the stabbing, but he had so much to cover that I didn't get the chance. It was good anyway for the two of us to be out like that. I appreciated the company.

'It's not what you did with Nicola that counted,' I said.

'We are damaged by what we do, Marcus. What's done to us makes no difference.'

'It's not even what you did, but that you invented

Katie, invented the emotion. You feel bad about wasting all that time.'

'So it should have been Nicola?'

I was saddened that he was really listening, really hoping I had answers.

'Maybe neither. For fuck's sake, Patrick. What if nobody ends up with anybody? It's not your whole life.'

'That's easy to say when you're sleeping with my girlfriend.'

We laughed at that, and I thought perhaps he was finding a way out of all this introspection. Until we left the pub, I had no idea how badly things were going wrong for him. Whether he'd been drinking more than I'd seen, I couldn't tell, but as soon as we got outside Patrick went down on his hands and knees, throwing up, gently at first, then in a rush. It was mostly liquid, and it came out like a bucket being poured. Whenever I see that, I think of the way they show vomiting in films; people make a lurching sound, cover their mouths, then cough. At best they give out a mouthful of slush. In reality, there's usually minimal coughing, and your hands go to the floor rather than your mouth. There's a sound similar to the one a sleeper makes waking from a falling dream. The sheer volume that slaps on to the pavement makes those film vomits seem trivial by comparison. There was no resistance from Patrick, and I even felt he was giving it an extra push. He managed to avoid getting vomit on anything but his hands, but where it contacted his skin it had begun to stink.

'I think we should just go,' I said, because it had started to rain.

Patrick stepped carefully with his head down, giving in to the alcohol. Nothing was said, apart from comments on the cold and the state we were in. The ground felt slippery, as though the rain was freezing, and my thighs had that ache from drinking, which makes getting home feel like too much effort.

He insisted on taking a short cut, and headed across an empty, brightly lit car park. I followed him, but found it difficult to keep up. Approaching the centre of town, I could see a group of deaf people crowding around the entrance to a nightclub. It was one of the bigger clubs, the queue behind them going back as far as the nearest church. Somebody was speaking clearly on their behalf – he might have been a friend of theirs or a carer, I couldn't tell – but the deaf people were all making sounds. Those who could speak were shouting obscenities; the rest were just making noises. Every few seconds, the bouncers would speak into their radios then urge the crowd to get back.

Patrick stopped to watch, and although I tried to move him on he kept looking back that way.

'It's fire regulations, mate. Tell 'em,' the smallest bouncer said. 'If an alarm goes off and they can't hear it, then what? We get the blame when they burn to death.'

'Fucking cock,' Patrick shouted, but it was lost over the other voices. The queue was getting rowdy now, wanting to get out of the drizzle. I wanted to get as far away as possible in case it kicked off.

Patrick paused, leaning against a wall. He gripped his hair at the front, as though he was going to pull it out, and closed his eyes. I urged him to keep walking, but he knocked me away.

Police vans drove past, pulling up across the road from the club, and that seemed to trigger something. From where we were standing, I couldn't see who had attacked whom, but before the police had even climbed out, the club entrance was a mass of limbs. For the first few seconds it was quiet, but then they began to make noises, some just of exertion, others as they were thumped. The howls they made were almost inhuman The bouncers had managed to get back inside and close the doors as the police moved in.

I swore, but there was no response from Patrick, and I realised then that he'd gone. Hoping he'd just needed a piss, I went looking, walking quickly. In each street I could hear the echo of the fight, deep screams of anger growing distant.

Over that, in the other direction, I heard somebody screaming one long note. It was so shrill it must have torn his throat, and from the way the sounds moved he must have been sprinting. It could have been Patrick, but I wasn't up to running. I had to do something, though, because the noise he was making would get him arrested or beaten up. At the time, I didn't consider the emotional damage he might be doing to himself by getting so worked up.

The street I went down was narrow and cobbled, with no lights, but there was enough of an orange cast to the clouds for me to see where I was going. I couldn't tell whether he'd gone down the alley or out the other end, so I kept up my speed. Being drunk, I ran too fast and felt almost buoyant for a second before I fell. I don't remember going down, and the impact was over before I knew what was happening. As the pain softened into my hands, I heard the screaming again, quieter, running out of energy. I needed help now, but he was moving away, leaving me to crawl over to the pavement.

Back on the main street, I looked at my hands, which were skinned and studded with gravel. You wouldn't think there were so many sharp particles on such a small piece of road. There was no blood, but my palms were glassy with the dew of lymph. Three lads came up to me, asking if I was in trouble. They had little heads and mean faces, the sort of hard bastards I wouldn't usually dare speak to. From what they were saying, they thought I'd been attacked and wanted some of the action. I'd never met them before, but they wanted to get revenge for me. I assured them I was fine, it was an accident, and that I was looking for somebody. As they left, one of them put his hands on my shoulders. 'Take care, mate,' he said. 'Go and see a dentist.' I didn't know that my face had touched the ground, but using a shop window as a mirror I was able to see what he meant. My front teeth were trimmed with black where the gum had broken. The grazes on my cheek, chin, forehead and nose were bleeding, and at that point they began to hurt.

Normally, I'd have been more upset by that, but looking down the street I could see the air had ripped. Where Patrick had been running, the dim light heaved.

Whether Patrick had actually released his stored pain as rage, or simply been in pain, I couldn't tell. The next morning I went to look earlier than was pleasant, still sore with a hangover. My face was barely bruised, but it smarted in the wind.

It took a while for me to be certain, but after about ten minutes I was sure that the streets had already been cleared. I followed the trail back, looking in all the places that Patrick had been. Where the space had been distorted, it had now healed. Approaching the Lamb, I could see Patrick's vomit, thinned out by rain, the only memory of the incident. The surprise was to see Patrick coming out of the Lamb, calm, wide awake. Ian was with him at the door — I could just make out his pale face and ginger hair. They spoke briefly, and Patrick walked away. I was in full sight and had no chance to hide, but he didn't look in my direction, although I thought that Ian probably did.

It was possible he'd simply been clearing up his own mess, but that didn't ring true. Pain had been going missing from the Lamb, periodically, and it was the first place we'd seen the hollow distortions. I couldn't be certain he was raiding pain, but given his change of mood I didn't feel secure trusting him. I suspected that he might be heading straight to Katie's, but I wanted to speak to her first. If he was involved with something unusual, I had to be the one to bring her on. We'd taken too long approaching her, getting sidetracked with Patrick's desire, and it was time to move the process forward before she lost sight of her ability.

I found a phone box that smelled remarkably clean, perhaps because the lower windows had been kicked out, so that rain could wash out the worst of the piss. I was nervous calling Katie's number, hoping I wouldn't be seen.

It was still early, but she was already up. I asked her if she'd seen Patrick since last night, but she said she hadn't.

'Is something wrong?' she asked.

'No, but I've been a bit worried about him. We can talk about that more some other time. But I have to make some things clear first.'

'That sounds ominous.'

'No. It's just that I have things to show you.'

'I don't know what you mean.'

I waited a moment, wondering how transparent I should make my explanation.

'There are things we can do,' I said.

I could hear her breathing, and then she said, 'Do you mean things we can do together? I don't follow you.'

'I've been wanting to show you for some time. There's more going on here than the obvious.' She didn't reply, so I hoped it was starting to sink in. 'You haven't seen what's been offered you.'

I hadn't made anything clear, but she said, 'Show me then.'

We arranged a time to meet, and I walked home in the drizzle, feeling anxious, hoping I could get through the day without having to see Patrick.

It's easy to describe the rage as all-consuming, because it's so violent you feel that you could break your bones or scream yourself mad. Despite this, a part of your mind remains unaffected. It's the same part of you that observes for a long time, slowly and in detail, while you're crashing your car. The same part that judges rationally when you are arguing, knowing what a fool you look. When the mind begins to work faster, it produces the illusion of slower time. As a victim of the rage, you experience this dulling of time, so that within the fury there is a calm observer. Although people talked about losing themselves to the potency of rage, it was the remaining fragment of self that enabled them to refine the pain. It took a decision to let go of the anger, so that it could pass through, cleansed, an offering to the others.

I had to ensure that Katie would be taken into the momentum of rage, but the amount of pain I was carrying was more than you'd usually spend on a beginner. If I released it steadily, however, the trauma would be bearable. The tradition was to offer no instruction, because if a first-time victim is muddled with thoughts, the pain adheres to them and release is impossible. Being the victim would be confusing for her, but it was the only way I knew of to initiate a newcomer.

That night, I walked to the Crown and waited outside for Katie at dusk. She arrived fifteen minutes later, parked round the back and came out to meet me. It was dark by then, but in the glow from the pub I could tell that she smiled briefly. She didn't ask what I had in mind, but walked with me to the airfield, which was deserted at that time of night. The moon was a day past full, a black curve shaved off its edge. It gave enough light to make the grass look glossy, and to cast shadows from the control tower and hangar. The only colour came from the blinking red light on the tower's aerial.

As we approached the clubhouse, she stopped. The building looked dark, its windows black.

'Is this all a part of it?' she asked.

'You know what's happening then?'

She looked at me again. 'I have some idea.'

I tried not to look too surprised at her perception, relieved that her initiation would soon be over.

'Are you going to show me in there?' she asked, pointing at the clubhouse.

It was easier to take her inside than to respond to that, so I walked over, unlocked the door and went in first. There was no need to turn on the light, because the floorboards were polished with moonlight. Katie stepped inside, and I shut the door behind her. The volume lessened; my breathing was laboured, but as the silence developed it sounded like the breath of sleep.

Pushing the table aside, I encouraged the silence further, and Katie must have noticed because she tilted her head as she watched me. She stayed close to the door, her arms folded. With the space clear, I placed one chair where the edge of the circle would have been if we were all present. My footsteps on the hollow floor sounded far away, and when I told her to come closer I could barely hear my voice. She didn't move, but I willed her to come into the middle of the room.

She wrapped her arms tighter, so I held out one hand to her. She took it, and I moved to the middle; her grip was so light that there was no sense of pressure or drag between us. When she was in the centre I let go of her hand, sat on the lone chair facing her, and completed the silence.

I brought the threads forward, the sensation making me heady, and I knew that the look on my face must be disturbing her, so I tried to let the pain move out of me. The pressure built, my skin straining across my chest and neck, but the pain lodged there, making my throat narrow. As I struggled for breath, I was also aware of Katie's rapid movement from her place in the centre. She was supposed to keep still, but went to the side of the room, never taking her eyes off me. The reflected gloaming matted over her eyes, hiding her pupils in a sheen of white. She picked up another chair, pushed it in front of me and sat there, calm in an instant, hands placed on her thighs, palms upward.

My spine felt like it was being stitched with wire, my ribs pushed out, pulling at my sternum. I was too distracted by the scrape of pain to realise exactly what Katie was doing, but then she put her hands together on her lap, rubbing them in circles. She widened her eyes into a black stare, her mouth open in a grimace, cheeks tense. I tried to speak and my larynx vibrated, but silence took the words. I felt as though I'd been winded, and found myself leaning forward. I heard coughing, as the sound returned, and knew it was my own.

I managed to stand, and kicked my chair aside to break the circle. It moved quickly, but as it tumbled on to its side by the wall, it slowed, falling gently to rest.

I went down, and my hands were wide on the floor, looking whiter than was natural. Craning my neck up, I saw something dark coiling out of Katie's solar plexus. A fibre of pain reached out from her and touched me. I bit my tongue, the vast breaths I made forcing blood to drizzle between my teeth as the rage enveloped me. My bones felt heavy, muscle banding around them. I tried to push the pain back at her, but she moved her head towards me, teeth gritted, forcing it into me.

My view of Katie was unclear, but I could see that she was describing signs with her fingers. It looked like she was trying to get hold of something. Her arms traced lines, and she was speaking words that I didn't recognise, each barked out like a command.

Amid this observation, a small thought formed. Katie was making me her victim while I was already swollen with stored pain. I wouldn't be able to release whatever was within me. As the last of her thread snaked into me, it combined with my own disorder and fattened. This could be why her flowing gestures had no effect, even though they became more frantic. Her ritual failed, and she stepped back, fingers pressed into her temples. She made an anguished sound, a sustained, rattling groan.

The mass of threads felt unsteady, and I worried that

they might damage me. In that moment of fear the pain erupted from me.

When you see slow-motion film of a drop of water splashing into a pond, there is a moment when the surface becomes spiked, like a crown, each pin of liquid releasing another drop of water. When the distortion spread from me, it looked like that for a second, then inflated, each tendril warping.

There was a smell of petrol, and something sweaty, like onions and hair. The feeling was similar to the few seconds of dizziness that occur when you're about to faint or be sick, except that it went on and on. My body must have slumped because my face was pushed against the floorboards, tongue touching the wood, skin pressing into the cracks. I heard footsteps go past me, felt cold air from an open door, but was unable to stir myself to follow her. All that I could do was watch my breathing, making sure it continued, trying to ignore the fever wetting my clothes.

As the shivering relaxed it became obvious that several hours had passed, because dawn was under way. I was slumped where I'd fallen, and felt as though I'd blacked out rather than slept. Standing up, I could tell there was no permanent damage to my body, but felt as though I had flu. The sky outside was busy with seagulls, their call closer than usual. They used low air currents to soar over the grass at speed, their shadows flashing up the window opposite to the direction of their flight. The clubhouse door had been left open, the wind pulling it, never enough to click it shut.

The distortion creased the air in the clubhouse and was easy to see even in daylight. Its base was the size of the circle used in rage meetings, but higher up it widened, arms branching out, passing through the walls and ceiling. The potency of the disruption was unnerving, and I didn't want to linger near that uncleansed pain, so I stepped out of the clubhouse and locked up. Even at a distance I was aware of its weight behind me. The feeling reminded me of those days when I'd been in a bad mood without knowing why, disturbed by a constant moodiness. Even when I tried to think about the simple practical steps I should take, the mass of the distortion nagged at my thoughts. It occurred to me that so much pain, matted together in the place of our workings, could damage the town if we didn't contain it soon.

It took a conscious effort to relax my face, because I was frowning. I tried not to feel betrayed or to take Katie's actions personally. It was more important to find out what was going on and try to stop her doing any more damage. There was also a chance we would need her help in containing the vast distortion. It was upsetting, though, that she had left me on the floor, and I wanted to put that down to her fear rather than to any malice.

I considered using the payphone at the base of the control tower to contact Donald or the others for help, but felt guilty for having triggered this problem. It would be best if I could find a way to sort it out on my own, before they knew. Most of all I wanted to talk to Patrick. I was weary, and felt as though I'd been crying in my sleep.

It was too windy for there to be much flying, but Donald would be along soon to work the tower, and I wanted to leave without being collared by him. I walked to the edge of the airfield, climbed over the fence, and walked behind the dunes past the back of the Crown. It was more difficult than I'd thought, trying to get home while avoiding the main roads, passing over unused ground. With no paths, the going was slow. Walking away from the roads reminds you how remote an island it is; the built-up areas are sparse, set among miles of grassland. You get the same impression from the air, when you see the streets as threads through an island of grass, but as soon as you're back in civilisation you forget the surrounding wilderness.

Cutting across the playing field at St Leonard's School, I realised it was later than I'd thought, because I could hear children singing. That would make it somewhere around mid-morning. I looked into the school's main hall, where the choir was lined up. The sound of the practice had sometimes carried as far as my house, but I'd never heard their voices so close, so I paused to listen. Choral music makes humans sound supernaturally pure, and the effect is more startling with children. I couldn't reconcile the sound with the hard-faced kids I'd passed outside the school in previous weeks. The song ended, and an adult figure came to the window, looking my way, hands on hips. I moved quickly on, climbing over my fence and going in through the back door.

Patrick didn't come to the door when I knocked, but I couldn't tell whether he was out or asleep. I still wasn't happy about the way he'd reacted the other night, but given Katie's revelation I was now more inclined to trust him. If anybody had been stealing pain and corrupting it, she was the one. Unwilling to stand there any longer, I headed to the centre of town again. I pictured myself meeting Patrick, and hoped that my walk would lead me to him. That was a mistake, because the technique requires trust if it's to work. When you hope for something, a part of you doubts that it will happen, effectively negating trust. Having made so many mistakes with Katie, my confidence in my abilities had diminished, leaving me with little faith. At the road junction I found myself thinking about the best route to take, rather than choosing a direction by feel. It was the first time that had happened in over a decade.

To avoid feeling the disorientation again, I set myself an overall direction, heading for Suzette's. I wouldn't be able to tell her what was going on, but the thought of sharing breakfast with her was comforting.

Barrow was heaving, slowing my progress through to the other side. On Margaret Street there was a crowd around an ambulance. From what I could tell, a car had crashed, mounting the pavement. There was a flash of red blankets, calm voices. Nearby, two dreadlocked travellers were arguing with a middle-aged woman. They drank beer from cans in between snapped comments, but still looked like boys being told off by a teacher. Both stood with a sag in their posture, knees bent, shoulders slumped in their big, holey jumpers. Their bony dog tugged on a lead made from a rag of pink blanket. It was rare to see such conflicts, and I worried that the equilibrium of the town was being disturbed. The argument seemed to diffuse when the ambulance drove away.

Further down, outside Woolworths, a scruffy man was crouched by his child, holding a fist up at his face. The boy looked about five years old, smart and clean, but the man was grubby, his hair unbrushed, face greased with stubble. The only clean thing about him were the earrings in his left ear. He tapped his knuckles on the child's cheek, his face quite passive as he said, 'If you do that again, I'll knock your fucking teeth out. I mean it.' The child looked down, but didn't cry as I'd expected. I'm not a violent person, and I rarely interfere with people, but I was tempted to kick the man over. I didn't want to hurt him, necessarily, but wanted to show him that he was wrong. I resisted, because I refused to succumb to the infection of his violence. The sad thing was that, although I could resist, his child didn't stand a chance. I said the word 'twat' as I passed, but he didn't even flinch.

Outside the Job Centre, people were sitting on the walls and benches, as though it was a park. Without exception they looked colder than they should have, their eyes underlined with bruise-coloured smears. A thin, exhausted woman with straggly hair was smoking fiercely, never pulling the fag more than an inch from her mouth. She watched a little girl chase the pigeons, raising a grim smile when the child almost managed to stamp on one.

Anxious to get to Suzette's, I hurried on. In the middle of the footpath was an old man on one of those electric wheelchairs that you sit across like a bike. He was wearing a grey polyester coat; I couldn't see his face, just his bald, blotchy head. I tried to get past but he speeded up, moving across on me. Pedestrians coming the other way forced me to fall in behind him again. Each time I tried to get past, he swayed across, speeding up, the electric motor straining. When I settled to walk behind him, he reduced his speed to slower than my walking pace. I was about to get mad and say something when he took one hand off the control and waved me past, leaving me so little room I had to walk in the gutter.

As I approached Suzette's flat there was a man standing in the doorway smoking a roll-up. He was fat, with a set of tiny brown teeth like fragments of bone, eyes so glazed he appeared to have cataracts. He pressed her bell for me, then stepped from foot to foot, as though cold, while I waited for Suzette to answer. He looked up when a light aeroplane flew overhead, and I looked with him. Suzette must have seen me coming because she didn't ask who was there, but said, 'It's open, come up.'

I went upstairs and she opened the door, letting me in and closing it behind me. There was no kiss, because she said, 'Are you looking for Patrick as well?'

'Has somebody else been looking for him?'

She nodded, yawning. 'That John character, with the glasses. He came over first thing, it was barely light. And then somebody called Ian – ginger hair, beard, dirty-looking. From a pub.'

'So have you seen Patrick?' I asked.

'Not for a long time, Marcus. Why would anybody think he would be coming here?'

'I don't know.' It was possible John and Ian were tracking him all over town, and this was one more place they'd thought to try. John, at least, would have sensed what had happened at the clubhouse and would want to know what was happening.

'Well, if he comes over, can you tell him that I'm looking for him? I'll try his house tonight. But if anybody else asks, don't say I was here.'

Unable to contact the owner of the Arcadia Bookshop, I resigned myself to losing my job, telling myself that my real responsibility lay elsewhere. With that decision made, I went to the Lamb, but the door was locked. After a couple of minutes' knocking I realised that Ian had chosen to keep me out. I assumed his father was back in hospital and his mother staying with relatives, but I felt certain that he was indoors. His refusal to let me in was an admission of guilt and made me determined to get hold of him.

I went through the archway into the car park at the back, tested both doors, the toilet and kitchen windows, and accepted that I would have to break in. It's not something I'm fond of doing, unless it's of benefit to the owners, but I could make an exception. I wasn't particularly good with locks, but it would be too much trouble to seek out an accomplice. I wanted to approach Ian alone. The fewer people who knew the details of my problem, the calmer I would be.

After another brief attempt at knocking on the ground-floor windows, I resigned myself to causing damage. I dragged an aluminium barrel from between the Coke crates, debating whether to lob it at the kitchen window or use it to climb to a higher level. Losing patience, still troubled by weakness, I opted for the former. The barrel was heavier than it looked once hoisted to chest height, but that meant it passed through the glass easily. The noise was much louder than I'd expected, and it carried on for several seconds as loosened shards fell among those already fallen.

It took me a minute to arrange crates beneath the ledge and to climb through without being sliced. I began to wonder whether Ian was in, because no matter what Katie had been up to the noise should have attracted his attention.

The internal doors were unlocked, making it easy for me to get into the private part of the building. I was working out which would be the best way to get to Ian's room when I found him in the hall. He was naked, apart from a wet towel, the same sallow colour as his body. The hall was all dark wood and red wallpaper, the only light coming through frosted-glass windows above the main door. The glow made his skin look luminous, despite its sickly hue. One hand gripped a bulge where the material of his towel joined up over his groin, the other was held out, palm facing me. At first I thought he was urging me to leave or be quiet, but his face had the sorry expression of somebody about to be slapped. He was trying to calm me down, and when I stepped towards him I was pleased to see that he was afraid. This could give me some leverage.

'Is she here?' I asked.

He looked so confused I thought something had been done to keep him quiet. His beard was wet, clogging in curls, and he licked at the edge of them.

'Is she here?' I said again.

He uttered something that sounded like, 'I'll get what I deserve', and backed off again until he was at the base of the stairs.

'I'm not leaving until you tell me, so keep still.'

That had the effect of making him motionless, his muscles freezing into position.

'Your parents are out?' I asked.

'Mum'll be back soon.'

'Tell me what's been going on.'

'I can't.' There was a plea in his voice, making me think he was asking for my help, as though he was scared of somebody else. 'I just can't.'

Unwilling to wait for him to make sense, I went into the public bar, then the lounge, checking for damage. I didn't take as much time as I could have, but it was clear that the pub was free of pain.

When I went back into the hall, Ian was in the same place, waiting.

'Either the pub's been closed for the past few days or you've been stealing from me.'

'Not me.'

'But you know who.'

I didn't want to put words into his mouth, but I needed a confession, so tried again.

'You let somebody take the pain?'

He gave a slight nod.

'Ian, did you think you could get away with this, without me noticing?'

I could see he was trying to think of some way to mislead me, but my intrusion had stunned him enough to confuse his excuses.

'Has she been here?'

'No. It didn't work.'

'What didn't work?'

I walked past him and went upstairs. The landing was built on several levels, each room at a different height. All the doors were ajar except one, which made my search easier. It was unlocked, so I went straight in.

His bedroom smelled of clothes and damp. The walls were a mess of posters and photographs. Books were piled by the skirting board, and I had to step between mounds of laundry and magazines to search the place.

If it wasn't for my background I could have missed the devices in Ian's bedroom, because they were simple. The general clutter of the room meant that the few ornaments he kept were clustered together on the windowsill. A jam jar, filled with water, had an onion growing in it. It could have escaped my attention, except that I saw a distortion shaping the air around it. Its roots were as white as rice, new shoots breaking through the ginger shell. Around the base of the jar were five stones, ordinary enough to have been taken from any beach. When I looked closely, I saw that circles and lines were scratched on to them. Around these, traces of salt.

Ian stood in the doorway, and I was tempted to smash his jar against the wall, or to throw it at him, but instead I let him watch as I put my hand into its puny energy and charmed it away. The onion wouldn't look any different to him, but he knew what I had done.

Sitting on the bed, I invited him next to me. I don't know why he thought I could be violent, but he was afraid. It was possible that he'd been told I could hurt him in other ways. Over the years, his awareness of my search for pain may have been off-putting, making me appear more sinister than I intended to be. He sat beside me, looking at his knees, his beard and hair congealing as they dried.

'What did she promise you?' I asked, wondering what the device was meant to have been for.

'I don't know.'

'Ian, I know you let her take the pain, in return for this,' I said, pointing at the jar.

He rubbed his face, the hand coming away wet. 'I don't know who you mean.'

'Katie Oswald.'

'No.' He shook his head rapidly. 'She was for Patrick. I wanted . . . somebody else.'

It wouldn't matter if I looked shocked, because if it came down to it I could frighten any information I wanted out of Ian; but I tried to stay calm, not for the sake of secrecy but because his words were a surprise.

'Patrick set this up?' I asked, pointing at his crude altar.

'Yes,' he said, his tongue sounding sticky.

'You'd better explain this.'

'We agreed to work together months ago,' he said quickly, as though making the confession eased the tension. 'I let him come in after closing time, every now and then. That was all. He did some of your work, not all of it. But then he wanted more and more time; he spent longer here, doing different things.'

'And what was the deal?'

'He offered to share some of the . . . produce.' He looked at the onion, and I knew that Patrick must have offered to put a trace of the energy into Ian's working. I would once have found it laughable to think that such a physically orientated ritual could have a strong effect, but now I wasn't sure. Patrick's secret had upset me in itself, but to know that he was also encouraging this type of practice was a worry.

'Was he instructing you?'

'Sometimes. I went to his house sometimes, and he showed me things.'

'When he was here, did you see exactly what he got up to?'

'Not always. Sometimes it was noisy and lasted for hours. He took advantage of my mum and dad being out of the way.'

'Was Katie ever with him?' I asked.

'No. He wanted to keep her out of all this.' Once again Ian had surprised me. Until now, I didn't think he knew any of my business, other than where it concerned his pub. To find that Patrick had been confiding in him put me off balance, and I had to force myself to listen to the rest of his words. 'I don't know what went on between them. But I don't think Patrick has been able to get near to her again. It wasn't working.'

From that, I gathered he didn't know much more than he'd picked up from Patrick's veiled comments. Ian clearly had no idea that Katie had been involved as well, with or without Patrick. While I had him off guard, and before Patrick could speak to him, I had to get as much information out of Ian as possible. I told him to get dressed, to make him less nervous. He turned away, perhaps thinking that the sight of his backside was less offensive than a full frontal. When dressed, he explained everything as he knew it, pausing over aspects that he didn't understand, trying to make his betrayal of me sound less deliberate, suggesting coercion, repeating aspects of his weakness. His story was confused by mistaken beliefs about our system, and from what I could tell Patrick had exaggerated our abilities. There was never any promise that Ian would be initiated into the rage, but he would be allowed to perform his own ritual. That was why he'd turned against me; Patrick had offered him something in return, when all I'd done was tell him to keep quiet.

'It wasn't personal, Marcus. I just wanted something to actually happen. In my life.'

'What did you hope to gain?'

His lips went pale, wobbling as he explained. He said a girl's name, nobody I knew, but made it clear the ritual had been an enchantment.

'It was the same for Patrick. He was trying to make Katie aware of him, but it was getting out of hand. Something went wrong the night before last.'

'How do you know this?'

'Patrick came round this morning, about two hours

before you. He made me let him in. Then he went round the whole place, moving from room to room, furious, chanting something. I couldn't make it out. There were other sounds. And then he said something of his had been stolen. I couldn't get much sense out of him. I just kept out of his way until it was over.'

'And he was alone?'

'Yes.'

'There was no sign of Katie?'

'No.'

I told him to think carefully, to remember whether anything had ever been said, about where Patrick might go in an emergency. He couldn't think of anything. Fear might have kept his mouth shut, if Patrick had threatened him, but he was so malleable I imagined he really didn't know the full story.

'Can't you find him,' he asked, 'with your...?' He made a spiral gesture with his fingers, probably thinking I could close my eyes and divine the answers.

'It doesn't work like that.' Although I could find out much more via the process of extended perception, such actions should be performed in the afterglow of rage. My concern now was that Patrick, as well as Katie, had found a way to get around this. They were applying the energy without the cleansing.

I stood up to leave, and Ian tried to sound upbeat, as though our conversation had been a friendly chat. 'So will you still be dropping in?' he asked.

'I will, once this is cleared up.'

He cried as I left, fingers wiping at his tears, his mouth and nose glossy with mucus running into his beard. I was tempted to stay and watch, because from the back of his neck a fine line of pain trickled up, making it look as though he was being hanged.

There was still no sign of Patrick at his house, and Katie's flat was locked with the curtains closed. I didn't think they were working together, as both had good reasons to be hiding. Patrick probably had no idea about the extent of her renewal, or that she was able to use it in such a directed manner. I suspected him of doing exactly the same thing, gathering an excess of pain and using it in ritual. I tried not to be frightened by that, because I didn't really believe it could work.

A quick visit to the closed-down shop made it clear that somebody had been there. I suspected it was Katie, because she was the one most likely to have been working in such a mannered way. The walls had been scratched, and the symbols smudged away. The lampshade, to my surprise, had been taken away. I hadn't realised until then that it had been anything other than a source of light.

Exhausted, I spent the rest of the day at home. I'd considered going back to Suzette's, but I'd have felt the need to talk, and that would be unwise. I felt tired and upset about the way things had developed. Worst of all, I was missing Nicola. We hadn't spoken since she'd slept with Patrick, perhaps because she had no reason to remain in touch. It was peculiar, though, because I wasn't missing those original emotions so much as her company. I didn't want to trouble myself with longing, but would simply have loved to spend time with her. She was one of the only people who made me look for the good in everything.

I slept until evening, and once I'd eaten I felt compelled to find more answers, even though it was getting late.

It was throwing-out time by the time I made it into

town, the pubs putting people on the street, where they continued to drink from bottles. Many were too skint for the clubs, but were reluctant to go home. Walking between pizza boxes and smashed glass was difficult enough, but it was made treacherous by men in white shirts leaping around with their arms out. They'd reached a state of drunkenness where they gained their entertainment from frightening passers-by. My temper was short, but I ignored them as I went past, and in response they made whooping noises.

It was cold and cloudless, but the stars were hidden by a haze of streetlight. I might have put my hands in my pockets for warmth, but at that time of night it would be unwise. Unprovoked attacks are common even in midweek, and if you walk with your head down and your hands buried, you're effectively asking for a kicking.

I managed to get to the town centre without any bother. The square was well lit, so it was easy to see the mess of litter and bottles, but I was struck more by the smell of beer and sick. Crowds were dispersing slowly, talking at pub volume, and their voices merged over each other so there were no recognisable words. It sounded like a moan, punctuated by shouts. You'd think with all that drinking going on there would be laughter, but even when I listened out for it, there was none.

Standing by the police vans, I took my time to have a good look around. There were several people I could have followed, had they been alone, but most moved on in groups or climbed into taxis. I needed a loner, which meant it would have to be a man. Even if I found a suitable woman, following her would get me into trouble and cause unwarranted distress. When the crowd was thinning, I thought it would be easier to find somebody alone if I went to a quieter area.

Somebody was singing a couple of streets away, each line ending with a wail, which became more angry until there was no song, only shouting. I ran to the top of the street, quickly passing the ends of other roads, trying to locate him. It was too dark to make anybody out, and the wind blew straight in my ear, making it difficult to hear his voice.

It occurred to me that I was trying too hard. You can't force these situations by chasing people down. If you stand quietly, away from view, the right person will cross your path. All I needed to do was stand and wait, knowing that the required person would appear. Ideally, I wanted somebody who was lost, but just about past caring. The cold keeps that type moving, which is better. If they once slump, you can't get anything out of them.

The man I chose was older than usual, being well into his forties, but thin. All his clothes were blue denim: shirt, jacket, jeans. He walked in bursts, pausing to steady himself before setting off again. Afraid of bumping into lampposts, he held his hands out as he passed them. He didn't see me as he went by, so I stepped out after him, walking as quietly as I could. He appeared to be ideal, because rather than singing or shouting he was muttering. I couldn't help but think that he was whispering secrets.

When I was close enough to hear him – the first audible words being something about a broken window – he stopped and turned to face me.

'Problem?'

To hear him speak so clearly was unexpected. I stopped walking, which made it obvious that I'd been following him. I should have carried on walking, telling him to calm down, making out that nothing was amiss. It would be difficult to distract him now.

'What's going on?' he said.

'Nothing mate,' I said, trying to look in the same state as he was, pretending to hold myself up against the air. It didn't convince him, and as I tried to get past he moved to stop me.

'No fucking way.'

It wouldn't have taken much effort to knock him down, but I backed off to give myself time to think. Being so drunk, he would be slow, and I wouldn't need to do anything other than fling him over. So long as he wasn't carrying a knife, I'd be fine. I was annoyed at wasting an opportunity, so in an attempt to recover the situation I told him to go home.

'You should have listened,' he said. I thought this was another threat, but saw that he was looking at the pavement, not at me. If he was talking to himself again, that was a good sign.

'Should have listened.'

'Listened to what?' I asked.

'You should have . . . listened to her . . . when she said.'

That was all I could make out, because his mouth was so full of spit he was unable to speak any more. If he once puked, there'd be no use for him. He leaned over, hands on his thighs, and I thought it was going to end there. He was panting to make himself recover, pushing his elbows against his stomach.

'I want to go home,' he said, looking up at me as though I was his friend. It almost felt like we'd been in town together for a drink and were helping each other to struggle home. He said it again, so I asked him where he lived.

'You should've taken me home.'

'Where do you live?'

He pointed, so I put my arm on his back and helped him to walk. It was the opposite direction to the one he'd been taking when I'd found him. Nothing else came from him for a while, because he was concentrating on pointing and balancing. We went back through the town square, glass crunching underfoot. It was colder, the pavement slabs textured with frost, except where people had urinated against the walls, their piss sticking in patches that refused to freeze.

I urged my companion to hurry up, trying to get him to stand straighter. He clung on to me as though he was my brother.

'Do you know where you are?' he asked me, when we turned on to the next street. His voice was clear again, the way it had been when he'd threatened me.

'Yes, it's all right.'

'Do you live around here?' he asked, but before I could answer he closed his eyes. He went down so heavily that he fell out of my grasp, his hands melting the frost. His jaw spread wide open, a watery line of mucus leading the way for gobs of hard vomit. It went over his hands and spread around them. The only sign that he was conscious, apart from his posture, was the way he spat between convulsions, getting rid of the wet crumbs clogging his mouth.

He got up and I backed away, because I didn't want him to hold on to me now that he was covered in sick. I doubted I'd get much more out of him, but wanted to make sure he was all right. He didn't respond at first, but managed to find a set of keys with his house number on them, which he handed to me. I walked ahead of him, looking for number 37, and he followed, holding his hands out as though they'd been burned.

Unwilling to go into the man's house, I unlocked the door and stood aside. He made it in, and when I tapped him on the shoulder to pass him his keys he looked at me as though he'd never seen me before.

'It doesn't mean *anything*,' he said.

If he'd said nothing, I might have been thinking that myself, because this divination seemed to have failed. His words, though, were so close to my thoughts, and alerted me.

'Is that what Patrick thinks?' I asked. 'Has he lost sight?'

'You should have told her,' was all he said before slamming the door.

The garden centre was contained in a strip of land between the rugby ground and the shops, with so little light the plants could barely grow. That's probably why they went in for so many cement fountains and terracotta kittens. The morning was bright, but the whole place was in shadow, with no sign of staff or customers. Wet trails of compost had been rained from shrub pots. There were no flowers to smell, only soil and rainy stone. It was the sort of place that couldn't decide whether it was indoors or outdoors, some areas half-covered with corrugated plastic, others left open. The only pretence of a room was the fluorescent-lit shop section, but even this had a wall missing instead of a door, making it feel too open. Unable to find John there, I headed for the Aquarium Centre.

The fish tanks were located in an unlit corridor, the only light coming from the illuminated tanks set into the walls, bubbling and stewing with fish. They gave off enough warmth to make it feel like a used bathroom. John was on his knees at the far end, removing weed and stones from an empty tank.

'What's bothering you, John?'

He screwed up his face, shaking his head. 'Nothing really. Just tired.'

'Has Patrick been worrying you?'

He shook his head more.

'I hear you were looking for him yesterday morning.'

'Do you have any idea what's going on?' he asked. 'Some of us went to the clubhouse yesterday, and saw . . . that thing. Don's livid. I've never heard him swear before, but he was ranting. The worst thing was that he looked scared. He wants to get hold of you and Patrick. He thinks you're hiding something from the rest of us.'

'It's not like that. But I need to lie low for a while.'

I explained about Katie as quickly as I could, telling him no more than was necessary. 'Does Don have any idea about her?' I asked.

'He never said so.'

'Did he tell you anything else?'

'He's terrified of that distortion. He wants it contained because of the damage it's doing.'

'I suppose that's understandable,' I said, looking back towards town. 'I've never seen the place in such a mess.'

'I know,' he said, screwing his eyes up in a worried squint. 'People seem more upset than usual.'

'Well, anyway, I need to borrow your car, if that's all right,' I said, and he immediately dug into his pocket for his keys. He asked no more questions, and didn't bother to tell me when he wanted it back.

'I'll put fuel in. I won't be going far.'

'Thanks,' he said, which made me feel like I was doing him the favour.

Once I'd got John's mini going, I headed for the coast. There were other places I could have filled up, but I let the Lucas garage be the augury for my direction. Fernleigh was standing by the cabin door, and waddled over as soon as he saw me turn in. The string-knit scarf around his neck looked grubbier than usual, and his skin appeared to be damp. I got out of the car and handed him the keys, telling him to put in two pounds' worth of unleaded.

It must have sounded a strange request, so I lied, saying, 'Just topping up.' Then I passed him the plastic can from the front seat, and asked him to fill it too.

The device in his throat made a spinning sound; I couldn't tell whether he was speaking or preparing to. It might even have been a sigh. He knelt by the plastic can, swishing fuel in, the fumes distorting the air. When the pump was back in the cradle, he stood in front of me and his throat hummed, his mouth shaping the words.

'Fhiffe-nhine-fhiffe.'

I gathered that he was asking for five pounds ninety-five, and fished it out of my pocket. His throat purred again. Holding one hand out, he drew a line down his palm and repeated the phrase, 'Fhiffe-nhine-fhiffe.'

The needle hadn't risen above the red line, and John's car was less than efficient, so I knew the fuel could run out at any time within the next half-hour. The north road led me on to the A595, around Silecroft Bay, where the road hugged the sea-level edge of Black Combe. The cloud was broken and the air misty, making the car feel hot and muggy. The road passed through villages that consisted mostly of corrugated sheds and caravans. Although there was evidence of farming, the only farm cottage I saw was set back half a mile from the road, hidden in the last clump of trees for miles. The route took me through inland cliffs, created by quarries, but the sea was always coming into view.

I headed inland, looking for familiar signs, trying to imagine how the place had looked at night, when Patrick had brought me there. The engine made a grumbling sound, then cut out. There was no gradual choking off, but an immediate shutdown. I dipped the clutch and let the car roll on to the grass verge.

There were no visible paths, but the ground rose away, so I waded through the grass and bracken until I reached a ridge. The ground levelled out there, with fields stretching out as far as the edge of the Lake District. I walked up to a barbed-wire fence and found a soil path alongside it. Walking down the path, I passed fields which had been set aside as stubble, and others which were greening, looking more like grass than wheat. The sun was behind me, making the landscape in front of me bright. Despite being overcast, there was a glare. A wired line of pylons were fogged into the background, the sag of their cables glinting like gold wire.

I could smell water and saw a banking to the north, which I guessed was a canal, but I followed the path's right-hand fork. It eventually led to a space where yellow gorse bushes lined both sides, and then it opened to another grassy area. There was a small building ahead of me, a short distance from the footpath, no larger than one room. Made from old stone and sloping tiles, it was windowless, and I could see no door. There didn't appear to be any path to the building itself, indicating that it had been long out of use. When I stopped, there was a sound like a hissing cistern, something clicking inside.

Looking up and down the path, I couldn't see any other buildings, or any reason for this one to be present. Whatever use it may once have had was difficult to guess. If there was a door, it must be around the other side, and it was this sense of intrigue that made me think about getting closer. I could climb over the barbed-wire fence and see if the door was open or locked. If it was open, there would be no harm in having a look inside. There was no one around. It would take less than a minute to get over, have a look and get back. It was such a minor trespass that I couldn't work out why I was being so hesitant. When I put my hand on the barbed wire to part it, I felt nervous. That was enough to make me realise the building was probably being protected in some way. Instead of worrying about getting in, I knew it would be best to concentrate on each step that I made towards it.

The grass around the building was more succulent than any I'd seen on my walk. It was so thick that my feet left imprints in it, the blades all combed in the direction of my progress. I knelt to touch it, and the feeling was like running my fingers through well-conditioned hair, it was so moist.

The door was around the back, unlocked, half-open, its wood warm to the touch. The brightness of the cloudy sunshine made it too dark to see inside, and I knew it would take a moment for my eyes to adjust. I didn't like the idea of being blind in there, so stood on the threshold. When I could make out the back wall, I stepped inside and the air cooled. Seams of light came in where the roof slates were loose against stones. The first shape I saw was a sink, its outside edge darkened by dust-filled cracks.

The interior of the bowl was clean, because water was running into it from a brass tap. There was no splutter, only the even seethe of water releasing into the plughole.

I touched the tap, putting my hands into the water, wondering how long it had been left on. When turned off, it stopped without dripping.

Looking further in, to the right, I saw that the floor was made of compact dirt. In the centre of the room was a person, kneeling like somebody about to be sick. The image was semi-transparent, more like a shadow, but I could tell that it was Patrick. He was circling his hands over the soil, and although there was no noise I could see traces of light beneath his fingers. His jaw was moving, but if he was speaking an invocation it went unheard. I didn't even blink, but the image spread, then vanished.

Whatever Patrick had been working on when he was there must have been completed long before I arrived, and he'd taken the useful residue with him. The afterimage was irretrievable, so I knelt to get a better look at the floor. Where his hands had passed, there was a circle of rough wax stains, each charred with the remains of wick.

I thought that might be as much as I'd find, but in getting lost on the way back to the car, I saw him. He was in an unploughed field, still golden with old straw. It was empty apart from one dead tree, which was lying on its side. It had decayed so there was nothing much other than a roughly hewn log. Patrick saw me but carried on with what he was doing, pouring petrol from a red plastic can. There was more urgency about his movements now. I never saw him strike a match or reach for a lighter, but flame moved along the log. Before I even got there, the petrol had burned away, barely charring the surface.

'I've lost track of what we're doing this for, Marcus,' he called. He looked calmer than I'd expected. He looked quite ordinary, like somebody trying hard to make something happen. Whatever he was trying to do, it was failing.

'We don't do it *for* anything, Patrick. Things don't always have a purpose.'

'But they always have a cause, don't they? Things don't just happen.'

'Sometimes they *do*. And causes don't always have effects.' I looked down at the log. 'At least, not in the way you intend them to.'

He put his hands on the bark, then gripped the log to pull it. He glanced behind him to the bank of the canal, weighing up how far it was.

'Conditions have to be met,' he said, struggling. 'Exact conditions. And then things can happen.'

'That's the principle of ritual, Patrick. You don't have to work that way.'

He didn't look convinced, but gave up pulling the log. He hadn't moved it anyway.

I asked him how he'd got here, and he said he'd walked from town.

'Because I didn't want to miss anything.'

He looked a bit lost now, uncertain of what to do next.

'Do you know what happened with Katie?' I asked.

'She came to?'

'On her own. She's doing things . . . I don't know what. I think she has been for some time. And I know about Ian, by the way.'

'Well, that's a relief,' he said. 'And you're still talking to me.'

'You look tired. You must be starving. Just give up on this.'

He looked at the sky, then across to the mountains. The air was misty, so that wherever the light shone – on wooden fences, pylons and distant rock – it was rosy, like copper. I could tell that he was seeing it for the first time.

5 Reflux

When we reached the clubhouse later that evening, it had burned down to a square of charred ground, flameless but smoking.

If you look at smoke with your back to the sun, it appears to be blue, but when you stare at the sun through it, the air is made slightly red. The colour was exaggerated because the clouds were trimmed with pink sunset, the sun at its reddest, about to meet the sea. There was enough daylight for the ashes to look white and cool, the embers glowing only when the wind caught them.

'Is this supposed to mean something?' Patrick asked, but I don't think he was really expecting an answer.

We talked a lot during that month. He told me that part of his problem was being uncertain about who to get over.

'I never know if I'm meant to be racked with guilt for being unfaithful to Katie or if I was meant to leave her for Nicola.'

'*Meant to?* What are you *on* about?'

I'd taken to being light, to stop him becoming too miserable. For the most part it seemed to work.

We walked to the southern end of Walney, on a path through the seagull sanctuary, between the down and fluff of nesting birds. I could smell broken eggs and the rotten bodies of the dead, laid out among the living. Some were fresh and intact, others hollowed by decay, the oldest nothing more than yellow, wet bones.

Looking north, I saw the Cherokee coming in to land, and wondered out loud who was up there.

We never found out what happened to Katie, or gained any further insights into her renewal. I'd have been willing to talk to her, but she never came back. That might be a good thing, because some of the others are less willing to forgive. In John's case, it isn't anger so much as fear. The last I heard from him, he was going out with Suzette. I'd split up with her before the flying season began. We reached that conclusion during a long night, neither of us being able to come up with a good reason. I don't think we were even sure whose idea it was. Just because something has come to an end, doesn't mean it's easy to sum up.

I'd imagined countless scenes where I'd tell Nicola that I loved her. In those fantasies she'd be so moved that she would open to the idea. Or, better still, she'd say that she had always loved me. There were many versions of this fantasy, but in some I'd build in a period of unrequited love, a temporary tragedy to hold off the resolution. In my favourite versions, I'd tell Nicola about that dream I'd had when I was fifteen. I'd tell her she was the one from the dream. Eventually, she would admit that she could remember the dream as well, and that would be that.

For a while I'd toyed with the possibility that she really could have been the one from my dream, but the truth was that I couldn't remember. I knew that if I met somebody new and cared for them, I'd start convincing myself that *they* were from the dream.

It would probably make more sense to tell her about the dream I had the night after we met. It would sound mundane in comparison, because nothing much happened. It's just that she was older, and more beautiful. I never knew whether I was even with her in that dream, but I still knew her, which was something.

Fantasy can have its uses, but I prefer to stay in the moment, observing what's going on. Heading down the airfield, though, I went over those images again, because I was finally going to tell her how I'd felt. I knew there would be no significant moment or reciprocation. It was more likely that she'd be frustrated that somebody else wanted her sexually, but I'd reached the point where it didn't matter.

It was a sunny morning, and Nicola was standing by the Flight Briefing Office, watching one of her students fly solo circuits in the Tomahawk. There was enough warmth to melt the frost, but the grass and tarmac were sopping with dew. The student's landings were far from three-pointers, but they were safe. I waited a distance away until the aircraft taxied off the runway. I'd only have a few minutes while he tied it down, but that would be enough.

'First solo?' I asked, as I walked up.

'Second,' she said. 'We've just been waiting for the right conditions. So how are you?'

She knew what was coming before I said anything. I could see it in her face.

'I'm fine, but I wanted to talk.'

The student parked the aircraft and cut the engine. It

was quieter than I'd have liked, and I was standing close to her. It had been a long time since I'd seen her in sunlight.

'Is this about Patrick?'

'No, it's about me.'

She was silent, and I knew not to speak. Whatever I'd imagined, I'd never pictured it like this. I wasn't even having to say anything. She knew what I meant, and actually saying that I loved her would be going too far.

'And now?' she asked.

'I still feel it, but I don't believe it any more.'

'Don't go just yet. Hang on a minute.'

Her student had finished with the aircraft and came over, grinning, hands full of headphones and logbooks. She went inside with him, and I was left there for about ten minutes. It got colder, and I paced. When she came back out, she stood further away, this time facing me directly. She didn't look angry, but startled. Her voice was quiet.

'Why tell me now, Marcus?'

'I've wanted to tell you for a long time, but given the way you were with Patrick . . .' She closed her eyes as I said that. 'I thought you'd probably stop seeing me altogether. I liked being around you too much to lose that. And I wouldn't have just been asking you out. I'd have been telling you that every moment you were around, moved me. That whenever you were in a room I spent most of my time trying to look elsewhere, because I didn't want to bother you.'

She said, 'You never bothered me.'

'But you knew?'

She looked up, shaking her head in uncertainty.

'If I said I felt the same, what would you do?'

'I don't think you feel the same,' I said.

'You know how Katie was, with Patrick? I don't think she loved him, or even liked him, but you can't be stared at for that long without it having an effect.'

'You think she was a victim of his emotions?' I asked.

'Not a victim, but you'd be so cold if you ignored such consistent passion.'

'Is that why you slept with him?'

'I was trying to hold on to a friendship, that's all. I thought if we got it out of the way he might stop wanting. Which he did.'

'That's probably just guilt,' I said, feeling cross that we were talking about Patrick.

Again I asked if she'd known how I felt.

'I don't know, Marcus. Perhaps.'

'Would it have made any difference if I'd told you sooner?'

'It might have done.' She pushed her hair aside, putting one palm on her cheek, feeling the heat there. Then she said, 'I sometimes think anybody would do, if they caught me in the right mood.'

I didn't want to believe that, but it made me wonder what I actually liked about Nicola. It was as though feelings had arisen and remained, no matter what actually happened.

'I dreamed about you the night after we met,' I said. 'That's probably all it was.'

There was a day in May when we were on the road above the park. Nicola stopped, looking down at the grassed area by the fountain. A group of teenagers were playing football, using trees for goals. Their ball was bright yellow and it made a subdued ringing sound when it was kicked.

Each time they hit the trees, it rained blossom. The petals fell slowly, like traces of afterimage, so that I almost thought there was something wrong with the air. Around their feet, there was a complete covering of petals, like soft, white ash. I don't think they even noticed.